The Falls

A NOVEL BY
JON GARCIA &
MARTY BEAUDET

BASED ON THE
SCREENPLAY BY
JON GARCIA

DSP PUBLICATIONS

Published by
DSP Publications

5032 Capital Circle SW, Suite 2, PMB# 279, Tallahassee, FL 32305-7886 USA
www.dsppublications.com/

The Falls
© 2016 Jon Garcia and Marty Beaudet.

Cover Design
© 2016 Paul Richmond.
http://www.paulrichmondstudio.com
Cover content is for illustrative purposes only and any person depicted on the cover is a model.

ISBN: 978-1-62798-984-8
Digital ISBN: 978-1-63216-317-2
Library of Congress Control Number: 2015945882
Published January 2016
v. 1.0

Printed in the United States of America

This paper meets the requirements of
ANSI/NISO Z39.48-1992 (Permanence of Paper).

The Falls

CHAPTER 1

I COULDN'T stand it. It had sat there unopened, propped against a vase of my mom's daffodils, since I brought it in from the mailbox. That had been hours ago, but it seemed like days already. I'd been checking that dang mailbox every day for, like, two weeks. It was my first stop when I got home from classes at the University of Idaho.

I'd been obsessing over that letter's arrival with a mixture of fear and excitement ever since I filed my mission papers. It held my future—a future directed by God's own prophet. It was the most important piece of mail I'd ever received.

And there it sat, unopened still.

I interrupted my pacing to stomp out to the back deck, where my mother was grading papers at the picnic table. "Mom, this is making me crazy. Can't I just open it?"

"RJ," she said, not even looking up at me, "you know we agreed the whole family would be together for this. After all, this call affects all of us, and we want to share in the excitement together."

We'd had this conversation before. My parents had both taken on extra work to help fund my two-year mission for the Mormon Church. Dad had started keeping his mechanic shop open on Saturdays; Mom would be teaching summer classes at Taylorville Middle School just down the street. And, as my dad liked to point out, my sister, Mary Anne, had willingly sold her car to contribute to my mission fund.

"Look, honey," Mom went on, "I'm not picking up your sister from soccer practice until six, and your father won't be home for another two hours. Why don't you go for a run? It'll help take your mind off it."

She was right. Thirty minutes later I was running north along the Idaho Falls Greenbelt Trail and the time was passing more quickly. I felt better already, with the sun sparkling on the surface of the Snake River to my left, and the temple coming up on my right. The temple. The very place I had entered for the first time just six weeks earlier.

It was a sobering moment when I was washed and anointed, and I finally received my temple endowment. The responsibility that came with that was scary, actually. It was a lot to live up to. Just a year earlier I'd given up on ever being worthy of a temple recommend, so it was hard to believe I'd made it to the temple at all. I'd had so much repenting to do, I thought it would be impossible.

But all of that was behind me now; I was done with my sinful rebellion. I was ready to become the faithful servant my patriarchal blessing promised me I could be if I remained obedient. I was an Elder of Israel, wearing the sacred garments, and I had received a calling from the Lord. A calling that sat inside that enigmatic envelope on the kitchen table.

Where would they send me? Spain? I'd had three years of high school Spanish. Latin America? The church was growing exponentially there. I'd be guaranteed lots of baptisms. Maybe they were sending me somewhere more exotic; I'd get to learn a new language at one of the Missionary Training Centers around the world. My mind reeled with the possibilities as I ran.

The answer, of course, was already written. The Lord's prophet had made the decision already. And as soon as I got home, my fate would be revealed. But that was still an hour away.

The late-afternoon sun was warm on my face. I slowed my pace and closed my eyes to soak it in. The light breeze felt good as it played across the sweat that trickled down my neck and shoulders. My calf muscles thrummed with that pleasant burn only running could produce. Mom had been right—a run was just what I'd needed. I felt alive and invigorated, ready for whatever the Lord had in store for me.

When I opened my eyes, returning from that brief reverie, I was surprised to realize I'd already jogged as far as Freeman Park. I hadn't meant to go that far. In fact, I'd vowed to forget that place and never return. Yet here I was. It was fraught with memories I'd made a solemn covenant to forget. I was instantly filled with regret.

Without hesitating, I reversed course and headed for home. I tried to focus on the temple ahead and banish the troubling memories that had returned so unexpectedly. I recalled Bishop Hunter's counsel: the Lord had forgiven me and forgotten. I needed to do the same.

When I reached the house, both my parents' vehicles were in the driveway, just as I'd hoped. *Yes!* The wait was over!

"Mom? Dad?" I called as I burst through the front door. "C'mon. Get in here!" I made straight for the kitchen table. "Mary Anne? Where are you?"

"Take it easy, son," Dad said with a chuckle as he came from the kitchen. "It's not going anywhere."

"Geez, Dad. I've already waited over four hours. The suspense is killing me!"

"All things are eternal unto the Lord, Ricky. It would do you good to learn some patience. This is a solemn moment. A turning point in your life. Don't you think it deserves some proper respect?" Dad gave me an affectionate pat on the back. When he pulled his hand away and gave it a conspicuous look, I decided I'd better go shower.

Less than fifteen minutes later I returned to the kitchen, still damp under my clothes. I didn't care; I'd barely paused to dry off. I made straight for the table where Mom, Dad, and Mary Anne were waiting, as though I was the one who was late. My parents' beaming faces barely registered as I grabbed the envelope and began ripping it open.

Dear Elder Smith, I read, *the Lord is pleased that you have chosen to serve in this great and glorious work.*

"Out loud, Ricky," Dad prodded. "Share the moment with us, son."

I repeated the letter's opening lines and hurried through the boilerplate content that had nothing to do with me personally. Finally I reached the nugget of revelation I'd been waiting for.

"The Lord has called you to serve in the Oregon Portland Mission of the Church of Jesus Christ of Latter-day Saints," I read aloud.

"Honey, that's wonderful," Mom enthused.

"Congratulations, son," Dad said, reaching over and patting me on the arm. "I know you'll serve the Lord well."

I did my best to share their enthusiasm. I smiled but said nothing as news of my fate sank in. Only my sister's expression seemed to reflect the disappointment I felt.

Portland? That was just one state away! Besides, how many people could I baptize in Oregon? Surely everybody there already knew about the church. There were already scads of Mormons in Oregon. What was the point of proselytizing there?

The look on Dad's face told me my forced smile wasn't cutting it. I'd have to try harder. I didn't want to seem ungrateful. It was the Lord who had made the assignment, after all. I needed to accept it with humility. "I'm so excited," I said, in an earnest effort to convince myself as well as my family. "I'm sure the Lord has some amazing experiences in store for me."

It sounded forced, even to me, but I really was trying. It would take some getting used to. The prophet had spoken: my future was to unfold only ten hours from home. There had to be a good reason. It would be my task to find out what it was.

CHAPTER 2

I STARED out at the vast expanse of the Great Salt Lake as the Greyhound hurtled down the I-15 corridor toward Salt Lake City and Provo beyond. I was glad to finally be on my way, even if it was only to the MTC. Three weeks of intense gospel study and preparation on the BYU campus still lay between me and my assignment in Oregon.

I had mixed feelings about that, which, if I was honest with myself, I did about so much of what lay ahead of me. On the one hand, I was excited to serve, to be part of that army of 60,000 young men celebrated for their devotion, sunny dispositions, and clean-cut good looks. On the other hand, I still questioned whether I was worthy to be counted among them. Not that I was bad-looking: tall; not overweight; I worked out regularly; I had a wrestler's build—I'd always thought my eyes were slightly too close together, though.

I was less certain whether I could fulfill the devotion and disposition parts of the equation. I'd always had to work at the dedication that seemed to come so easily to others. Not that it was intentional. I really did *want* to be good, but it was hard. I often got restless sitting through church meetings. My mind would wander; it was a constant battle to stay focused.

Priesthood meetings were the exception. They were the one place I felt special, like I was called to a higher purpose. Even so, I often felt undeserving of the honor. I found myself plagued by unworthy thoughts, even in that godly setting. What was wrong with me? Did others share my struggles? I wondered.

As for disposition, I wasn't outgoing like those I admired at school or in the ward; the ones who were always smiling and giving me a pat on the back. I worshipped some of those guys, but that wasn't my style. I'd never been the natural-born-leader type. I was uncomfortable being touchy-feely with people, especially other men.

In fact, I tended to be pretty much of a loner most of my life. I went out for wrestling and cross-country instead of team sports. And

I was good at them too. I had a dresser full of trophies back in my bedroom to show for it. I was proud of that, at least.

Like those trophies, everything familiar was behind me now, including my girlfriend, Elise. We'd been together three years, since the summer before my junior year in high school. We'd never done anything more than some kissing except one time, when we kind of did some dry-humping with all our clothes on. Elise, like most Mormon girls, had been prepared for my eventual mission and didn't complain when it was time to say good-bye. She cried, of course, and said she was proud of me. She was sure I would be the best missionary in the field and I would make our Heavenly Father proud. It was the same thing all the girls said about their missionaries. I wished I shared her certainty.

It made me uncomfortable when, the night before I left, Elise promised to wait for me. Maybe it was because girls who promised to wait for their missionaries to return rarely did. But who really knew what was going to happen two years from now? People change.

In fact, that was exactly why I wanted to go on a mission. I *needed* to change. There were things about myself I didn't like. Things Heavenly Father didn't like. Change was definitely on the agenda. I didn't know how or when it would happen, but I trusted the Lord had a plan for me. And when I returned I would be more like the men I admired. Somehow.

It was only a six-hour bus ride to Provo with stops, but by the time we rounded the Point of the Mountain into Utah Valley, I felt like I'd been in that seat for days. Brigham Young University wasn't exactly an exciting destination—I'd been there several times with my family for church-sponsored events—but now that I had a purpose, I was excited to be there and wanted to get on with it.

Three hours after I arrived, it was official: I was a missionary. I found myself sitting among a sea of nineteen-year-olds like me as the MTC president welcomed us into "God's Army." In spite of my fears and doubts, I couldn't help but feel proud as I scanned the faces of hundreds of other missionaries who shared my purpose. They were a handsome bunch, and I looked forward to the camaraderie and spiritual bonding that lay ahead.

I had finally left behind the competitive environment of high school, the trying to fit in, make friends, be liked, be cool. None of that mattered here. We were all cool now. We were set apart from the masses, literally, by the power of the priesthood. Petty differences had no place here. We were One. And it felt awesome.

After the general assembly, we were assigned to our respective districts and companionships for the three-week stay at the MTC. My district was made up of eight elders and two sisters; five companionships. We would all be assigned to new districts in the mission field once we reached Oregon, but for now we were a family.

My assigned MTC companion was Elder Huber, from Salt Lake City. I liked him immediately. He had a wicked sense of humor. He was blond, about my height, though really skinny. The rest of the elders in the district were a mixed bag: Elder Morehead was goofy; Elder Fields was kind of loud and obnoxious. It wasn't exactly the elite team I had envisioned when I set out, but I tried hard to look past the things that would normally bother me and remember that, whatever their shortcomings were, they, like me, had been chosen for a reason.

But it was the selection of Elder Rick Johnson as our district leader that seemed most inspired. Even though I'd only known the guy for a few hours, I was absolutely sure he was the best man for the job. He radiated warmth; his intense green eyes shone with enthusiasm for the work and love for his fellow man. He was full of energy and had a strong testimony of the gospel, which he bore to us that very first day. I immediately felt a strong connection to him.

Like the rest of us, Elder Johnson was only nineteen, but he had a maturity and confidence the rest of us, including me, lacked. He was also strikingly handsome—tall, rugged, broad shouldered. I was sure he worked out, as I did, which meant he had a respect for the earthly temple the Lord had blessed him with. I was fully behind Elder Johnson from the get-go. I looked forward to establishing a true bond of brotherhood, and I expected to learn from him how to be the man and the missionary Heavenly Father wanted me to be.

One day toward the end of our second week, Elder Johnson failed to show up for our afternoon Gospel Essentials class. I always enjoyed his contributions and looked forward to our frequent private discussions after class, and I was disappointed by his absence. When I asked Elder Fields, Johnson's companion, where he was, Fields told me he was in a meeting with the mission president. Though I missed our usual chat that afternoon, I accepted the fact that, as district leader, Elder Johnson had other responsibilities.

But when Elder Johnson also failed to show up for dinner that evening, I got concerned. Surely he wasn't still meeting with the mission president. I left the cafeteria—technically I wasn't supposed to do so without Elder Huber, but the whole place was full of missionaries, so what could happen?—and I went to Elder Johnson's room.

I found him there, also alone.

"Hey, there you are," I said, standing in the doorway. Then I noticed he was packing his belongings. "What are you doing?"

He turned and smiled, but it was a sad smile. "Hey, Elder Smith."

"Are you going somewhere?" I asked with more than a little apprehension rising, filling my gut. "Why are you packing?"

"I'm going home, Elder," he said, no longer looking at me.

"What? That's not possible. I mean, how... why... I don't understand." I walked over to the bed opposite him and sat, my knees already feeling weak.

"I don't expect you to understand, Elder Smith," he said. His tone was conciliatory. In spite of that, his words cut me to the quick. "I expect that a lot of people won't understand."

"But what happened?" I asked, almost pleading for an explanation. "How did this happen? Are you sick? Is there a family emergency?"

"No, no. I'm fine. Everything's fine."

"Then what?"

"I've been praying about this, Elder. And I finally got the answer: I don't belong here," he said, sitting down beside me on the bed.

"How can that be?" I asked, incredulous. "The Lord himself has called you."

"Well, not exactly," Johnson said. "His servants have called me, and they're not infallible; they do make mistakes once in a while."

Technically that was true, or at least what the church taught. But to start second-guessing something as important as a mission call was dangerous territory. I couldn't believe Rick Johnson would go down that road. "Maybe *you* made a mistake," I said, an unexpected anger creeping into my voice. I was feeling betrayed. "Maybe you misunderstood the answer to your prayer. Or maybe you were asking the wrong question."

"Elder Smith," he said, putting an arm around my shoulders, "like I said, I don't expect you to understand. This is a very personal decision. It's between me and our Heavenly Father."

His physical closeness, his gesture of fellowship, comforted and angered me simultaneously. When I spoke, tears began to flow. "Look, I don't know what you're struggling with, Elder Johnson, but whatever it is, you can overcome it. I know. I struggle too. But I'm not going to quit and you can't either."

"And I'm sure you'll succeed, Elder, and you'll be a fine missionary," he said, squeezing me even closer to him. "But it's not the path for me. I'm sincerely convinced of that."

I stood up abruptly and turned to face him. "Elder Johnson, I know the Lord wants you here. You've been an inspiration to me and the other missionaries in our district."

He started to respond, but I cut him off. "No, hear me out. Whatever unworthiness you feel about serving this mission, it can be no worse than what I have done. Just over a year ago, I had... well, I did something...." I searched for the words. "I mean, well, I was intimate with a man. With two men, even."

I'd never told anyone this before other than my designated priesthood leaders, and it was scary. I watched his face closely for a reaction, but all I saw was love. To my surprise, it infuriated me. How could he respond to me with so much Christlike love and yet quit on the Lord like this? "Elder, I repented and was deemed worthy to serve. If I can do this, so can you. Don't be a quitter!"

Despite my pleas, Johnson left the MTC the next morning. I felt personally betrayed, especially after opening up to him about my most personal of secrets. How could anything in his life be worse than that? Rick Johnson had been my mentor, my shining example, the man I wanted to become. And now he was turning his back, not only on the Lord but on all of us who had come to depend on him. How cowardly was that?

But even as I mourned his loss and indulged my anger, the real significance of his departure became all too clear to me: if someone as spiritual as Rick Johnson could fail, what did that say about my own prospects for success? Would I end up like Rick some day?

CHAPTER 3

"WELCOME TO the Oregon Portland Mission Home, Elders and Sisters. I'm President Pierce. I'll have a chance to chat with each of you before you're taken to your assigned areas later this afternoon to meet your new companions. But first Sister Pierce has prepared a nourishing lunch for us." He led the way into the dining room, where a table was set for ten.

I had been so nervous on the flight from Salt Lake, I hadn't even thought about food. Now the smell of beef stew, or whatever was in the large bowl in front of us, dredged up my suppressed appetite. I could hardly wait to dig in.

"Eat up," Elder Huber told me with a sardonic smile as he took a seat beside me. "This is our last civilized meal before they make us survive on our own cooking for two years."

"My cooking's pretty good, actually," I said. And I wasn't kidding; cooking was the one thing besides wrestling I was good at.

"Maybe it is," said Huber, "but remember, half the time you're going to have to eat your companion's cooking."

"I don't know," I told him. "I'm not going to eat just any old garbage. If he can't cook, then I'll just do all the cooking and he can do the dishes."

A little over an hour later, with a belly full of awesomely good stew, I was sitting in President Pierce's office for our introductory interview.

"We're pleased to have you in the Oregon Portland Mission, Elder Smith," he recited. His fixed smile and robotic delivery reminded me of a video game avatar. "The field is indeed ripe and ready to harvest. You have only to be diligent in your efforts and trust in the power of prayer, and you will be blessed."

"Yes, sir."

"Your first assignment," President Pierce went on, glancing down at a spreadsheet on the desk, "is to Clackamas Falls. Your trainer will be Elder Merrill."

I smiled, though the names meant nothing to me. I was just anxious to get there and finally get to be a real missionary. Three weeks of preparing and pretending had made me twitchy.

"Elder Merrill is one of our finest missionaries," the president continued. "His father is Noah G. Merrill of the First Quorum of the Seventy."

Wow. A General Authority's son, I thought. How would I ever be able to measure up to that? The guy was probably a spiritual giant who had memorized all the Standard Works. Man, the Lord was really gonna test me.

"That's great," I lied, doing my best not to let my apprehension show. "I'm sure I'm going to learn a lot from him."

"That's right, son. I like your attitude," Pierce said, standing and extending his hand. "Elder Harris, one of the Oregon City zone leaders, will take you to your assigned area now and introduce you. God bless you in your efforts."

Clackamas Falls, it turned out, wasn't that far from the Mission Home—only about a forty-five-minute drive. My first impression was that it seemed a lot like Idaho Falls, only smaller and with more trees. The Clackamas River wasn't as big as the Snake, but the falls themselves had a familiar feel. Elder Harris pointed them out as we drove by. I hoped maybe I'd get a chance to go running along the river like I did at home. Monday was preparation day—or P-day—the one day a week we were allowed to do personal things, like laundry, shopping, basketball, and writing letters home.

"Here we are," Harris said as we pulled to the curb in front of a large apartment building. He killed the engine. "This'll be your home for the next few months."

"Looks nice," I said, though I had no opinion of the place at all. It was a nondescript, brown-stucco, three-story building.

"Well, let's go on up and take a look," Harris said, popping the trunk and then stepping out of the car. I grabbed my two small suitcases from the back and followed him into the lobby.

The building was old, probably built before my parents were born; it smelled musty and ancient, mixed with fresh paint. The carpet on the stairs was stained, but nothing gross. I could have done a lot worse in some third-world country, I reminded myself.

Despite the shabbiness, it was exciting to be moving into my own apartment—the first time I'd lived anywhere without my parents. U of I had been within walking distance of home, so I'd never experienced dorm life until the MTC.

We reached the second-floor apartment; Harris gave a knock. There was no answer.

"Elder Merrill's out on an exchange with my companion today," Harris told me as he inserted a key in the lock. "They were supposed to be back by now." He opened the door and motioned for me to enter. "They'll probably be here any minute now," he said, following me inside. "Well, this is it," he said, waving an arm.

I looked around. A couple of beds, a nightstand, a desk, a dresser. A table in the kitchen. There wasn't much to it—it was just a studio. I supposed we didn't need any other rooms, though, since my companion and I were never supposed to be apart. Big windows let in what gray light there was from the overcast sky. I'd heard about the infamously drizzly days in Oregon. I noticed there were no curtains on the windows—probably because sunlight was so valuable.

"Oh, before I forget, here are your keys," Harris said. "The square one is for the main door. The other is for the apartment. This little one is for the mailbox."

"Thanks," I said. I set down my suitcases and took the keyring from him.

We stood looking at each other for an awkward moment.

"So," Harris said, regaining his momentum. "Bathroom. Closet." He pointed at each, as though I might have trouble identifying them without his help.

I turned the corner into the galley kitchen.

"Yeah. Kitchen in there," Harris narrated from the other room.

"It's perfect," I said, more to compensate for Harris's gawkiness than out of any kind of objective assessment. He was a funny little guy, nerdy, but in a clueless kind of way. I'd had plenty of geeky gamer friends back at school, but none were as socially awkward as this guy.

"Yeah. You'll like the neighborhood too," Harris added, pushing his glasses back up his nose.

I smiled and nodded. "I'm sure I will."

"So I hear you're quite the athlete," Harris blurted, apropos of nothing.

"I'm okay," I said with a shrug. I was more than okay, but there seemed little point in bragging about my wrestling trophies.

"Well, I've always heard it said, 'Don't be so modest, you're not that great,'" Harris said with a creepy smile.

"Uh, yeah," I said, wondering how this goofy guy got to be a zone leader. I looked away to defuse the awkwardness.

"So this is Elder Merrill's bed, and this one's yours," Harris said, again pointing out the obvious. "Keep it tidy."

I picked up my suitcases and tossed them onto the bed. Turning back to Harris, I said, "So tell me about Elder Merrill. What's he like?"

"His father is a member of the First Quorum of the Seventy. But I'm sure you already knew that. He reads a lot. He eats Lucky Charms like they're going out of style. I don't know...." He gave me a puzzled look. "Is there something specific you want to know?"

"No, I was just wondering."

Just then a missionary walked in the still-open front door. "Hey," he said as he walked past us and set his backpack on the dresser. "Good to see you, Elder Harris," he continued, extending his hand and shaking the zone leader's. He turned to me. "And you must be my new companion"—he glanced at my nametag—"Elder Smith, right?"

"Yes," I said, shaking his hand. "And you must be Elder Merrill."

"Yeah, that's me," Merrill said with a wide smile.

Merrill's red hair immediately reminded me of Rick Johnson, who I had mistakenly thought would be my role model. Now that Rick was gone, would this guy be the spiritual mentor I needed?

"So, did Elder Harris show you around a bit?" Merrill asked.

"Yeah, a little."

The conversation faltered. For a moment we all just looked at each other, smiling self-consciously. Uncomfortable, I looked down at my suitcase, then glanced back at Merrill. He was about to say something when we were rescued by the toot of a car horn from the street below.

"Well, that'll be Elder Schmidt," Harris said, visibly relieved. "I should let you guys get acquainted." He turned to me and said, "I look forward to getting your reports." As he headed out the door, he added, "I'm sure I'll see you around."

"Good-bye, Elder Harris," Merrill called after Harris. He gave me a wink, which pretty much told me he was thinking the same thing I was.

I turned back to my luggage and started unpacking, laying my unopened bags of temple garments and meticulously folded white shirts on the bed.

Merrill sat down and began untying his shoes.

"I have to tell you how happy I am to be here," I said, trying to sound like I meant it. I wanted to mean it, but I was more nervous than excited at the moment. "Very excited."

"Good," Merrill replied, glancing over his shoulder with a polite smile that only made me feel more self-conscious. I probably hadn't sounded convincing.

I tried again. "I'm looking forward to starting my missionary work." But it still sounded forced.

"That's good to know," Merrill said. He stood up and walked over to me. His smile seemed genuine now; perhaps I had misjudged him. He was probably a really nice guy.

"Would you like to start this companionship off with a prayer?" he asked.

"Yes. Definitely!" I said, and I meant it. That was exactly how we should begin. I could definitely use the Lord's help. I was pleased Merrill suggested it.

I bowed my head and began to kneel, but Merrill remained standing as he closed his eyes and started to pray. "Dear Heavenly Father—"

I caught myself just before my second knee hit the floor. I struggled back to an upright position, shuffling clumsily and interrupting Merrill's prayer.

He opened his eyes. "You all right?"

"Uh, yeah," I said, embarrassed. "Sure."

Merrill regarded me for a moment before returning to his prayer. He was probably thinking what a goofball I was. "Dear Heavenly Father, we thank you for bringing Elder Smith to join us in bringing souls to your church."

CHAPTER 4

ONLY WHEN the day's work was done and we were finally out of our suits and ties did we have a chance to talk about more personal things. We sat on our respective twin beds facing each other, eating Lucky Charms.

"Where are you from again?" I asked between mouthfuls. It was a stupid question, because I knew his dad was a GA. I was trying to get beyond the discomfort of sitting around socializing in my underwear, something I'd never done outside a locker room, so it felt kind of weird.

"Salt Lake," he said. "You're from Idaho, right?"

"Idaho Falls. Ever been there?"

"Yeah. Well, through it, at least. I mean, I think we stopped to see the falls on the way to visit our cousins in Rexburg," he said. "And I remember seeing the temple, but that's about all."

"Yeah, well, there isn't much else to see there," I said. "So you didn't miss anything."

Merrill laughed. As he did, a tiny bit of the cereal he was chewing launched from his mouth onto my arm. "Oh man. I'm sorry," Merrill said, reaching over and flicking it off.

I shuddered involuntarily at his touch. I wasn't sure why. Maybe it was the underwear thing. I felt kind of vulnerable and exposed. But, I thought, weren't missionaries meant to be close? We were companions, after all, twenty-four hours a day. And if we were expected to spend every waking moment together, it could get pretty intimate. In fact, President Pierce had counseled us to love our companions. So really, I had to ask myself, what was there to be uncomfortable about? The Lord intended for us to bond.

I had to laugh because Merrill was obviously embarrassed. "That's okay," I said. "I'm just glad it didn't land in my bowl. That would've been gross."

We both laughed, and I immediately felt more at ease.

"So, where were you serving before you came here?" I asked.

"Over on the coast. Seaside."

"Oh. Cool."

We continued eating in silence, and I began to relax. Everything was just as it should be. Heavenly Father had brought us together. Merrill wasn't a threat; we were brothers in the gospel, united in a noble cause.

"So what do you like to do?" Merrill asked, setting his empty bowl on the nightstand. "I mean, like, for fun."

"I like sports," I said, trying to sound like more of a jock than I really was.

"All of them? Or any in particular?"

"No. Well, I'm not bad at wrestling. I've won a few competitions."

"Wow," Merrill said in mock surprise. "Thanks for the warning!" He laughed. "And when you're not terrifying opponents, you do anything else?"

"I'm a drummer, yeah. And I'm learning—or I was learning—to play the guitar. I mean, it's not like I could bring instruments with me or anything."

"Yeah, that's against the rules, I guess."

"What about you?" I asked.

He hesitated before answering. "I don't know," he said with a shrug. "I guess I've been doing the missionary thing for so long… being a missionary is all I do."

"How long you been out?" I asked.

"I'm sorry?"

"In the mission field," I said. "How long you been serving?"

"Oh," he said with a smile. "Just over twenty months."

"Oh wow. So you've got less than four months left."

"Yeah. I guess so."

"Do you have a girlfriend back home?"

"No, fortunately," Merrill said. "You?"

"Yeah, her name's Elise. We've been together for a while."

"How long?"

"Almost three years," I said before slurping the last of the milk out of my spoon, something my mother would not have approved of.

Merrill was just staring at me. Maybe he didn't approve either. Or did I have cereal on my face? I wiped my mouth, just in case.

"Well, you got a picture?" Merrill said.

"Oh yeah. Sorry." I put down my bowl and grabbed my wallet from the nightstand. I pulled out my one picture of Elise and handed it to him.

"She's pretty," he said, handing the picture back.

"Thanks."

A few more moments passed in which we found nothing more to say. The silence was actually becoming comfortable.

"You done?" Merrill asked, picking up his own bowl and reaching for mine.

"Uh, yeah. Thanks."

When he returned from the kitchen, Elder Merrill said, "Okay. So I have some planning to do for tomorrow." He sat down at the desk and opened his planner. "We need to get you a bike, first thing."

"Yeah, I guess so."

"Listen," Merrill said, turning to me, "why don't you just go ahead and get some sleep. You've had a long day. You're still on Mountain Time. We can do this first thing tomorrow."

"No, really. I'm fine," I assured him. In reality I *was* exhausted, but I wanted to spend more time getting to know my new companion. "Are you sure you don't need my help with anything?"

"No, it's okay. You get some rest."

"Okay, if you're sure."

I got up and retrieved my toiletries bag from my suitcase. As I headed for the bathroom, Merrill called after me, "By the way, the left side of the dresser is yours."

"Thanks."

I flipped on the bathroom light, closed the door, and looked at myself in the mirror. I was now an honest-to-gosh missionary! I was both excited and nervous. Tomorrow I would have to go out and knock on my first door. *I can do this*, I told myself. *I've been set apart for this work.*

As I brushed my teeth, I replayed the day's events in my mind. I took comfort in the fact that whatever happened tomorrow, Elder Merrill would have my back. We were companions. It felt good to know that—reassuring. I could feel the confirmation of the Spirit that Elder Merrill and I had been brought together for a purpose.

CHAPTER 5

"GOOD MORNING, Elder!" I didn't remember what I had been dreaming about when Elder Merrill's greeting jolted me awake. I struggled to open my eyes against the blinding light flooding in through the large windows.

"Morning," I managed as I eyed the clock on the nightstand between our beds. It was 6:20. I'd overslept.

"You slept right through the alarm," Merrill said as he did hamstring stretches on the floor beside the bed. He was dressed in a T-shirt and running shorts. "I didn't have the heart to wake you earlier, this being your first full day and all. But you do know that our day begins officially at 6:00 a.m., right?"

"Uh, yeah," I said, swinging my legs out of bed and sitting up. "Sorry. I guess I was more tired than I thought."

We had gone over the schedule the night before. The mission had explicit rules about how we were to spend our time. A missionary who strayed from that schedule could be disciplined.

We were to be up at six to say our personal prayers, and then we were allowed forty-five minutes of exercise time. Fortunately Elder Merrill liked to run, so we agreed it would be part of our daily routine. Afterward we would shower, eat breakfast, and have our scripture study. We were expected to be out the door by nine.

It had sounded reasonable when we went over it the night before, but now I wasn't sure I was awake enough to run. As I wiped the sleep from my eyes, it occurred to me that Elder Merrill wasn't wearing his garments. "Are we allowed to go outside like that?" I asked, gesturing toward his running shorts. "I mean, without garments on?"

Something about his obvious athleticism—his bulging muscles, his raw physicality—made me uncomfortable. It seemed at odds, somehow, with the wholesome messenger-of-the-Lord image one usually associated with missionaries. Too visceral. Too worldly. Too studly. Missionaries weren't supposed to be sexy. In any case, it certainly wasn't what I had expected to wake up to.

"Sure," Merrill said. "Didn't they tell you when you received your endowment that you could take your garments off during sporting activities? You don't want them peeking out from under your shorts." He gestured at his muscular thighs.

"Well, yeah," I said, averting my gaze. "But I kinda thought that being missionaries and all, that… well, the bar was higher or something."

"Well, look, if it makes you uncomfortable—"

"No, no," I said. "It's fine. Just let me splash some water in my face." I stood up and trudged off to the bathroom. I would have to pray and pee at the same time to get back on schedule.

"You can borrow a pair of my shorts, Elder," Merrill called after me.

BY SEVEN thirty we had finished our scripture study and were digging into our bowls of Lucky Charms. I noticed there wasn't a whole lot of other food in the apartment, at least not for breakfast. No eggs or pancake mix. No bread for toast. Not even orange juice. Mom always had orange juice in the fridge. In fact, she rarely let me leave the house without having a glass, if she could help it. I used to complain, but now I missed it.

Elder Merrill was going over his planner. "Okay. Here's what we've got," he said around a mouthful of cereal. "We'll walk over to the Millers' house—that's about a mile and a half from here—and check out a bike for you. They offered it last Sunday at church when they heard I was getting a new companion."

"Great."

"It might be a little small, though. I didn't know you'd be so tall. I mean, it was their son's, and he was kinda short."

"That's okay. I'm sure it can be adjusted."

"Anyway," he said, turning back to his planner. "After that I thought we'd go out GQ'ing on Main Street."

"GQ'ing?"

"Yeah," Merrill said. "It stands for 'golden question.' You know, 'What do you know about the Book of Mormon? Would you like to know more?'"

"Wait. That's two questions," I said with a straight face.

"Ha-ha," he said. "You know, you're right. I never thought about that before."

We both laughed.

"Okay, so after lunch we'll do some tracting," Merrill continued. "Then at five we've got a dinner appointment with the Murdocks. They're all members, but Brother Murdock has been inactive for years. The bishop asked us if we could drop in once in a while."

"That sounds okay," I said.

"He's really a nice guy and all," Merrill added. "I think he just has a Word of Wisdom problem."

"Oh," I said. "Smoking?" Drinking and smoking were the two biggies for most people.

"Yeah. And drinking, I think. I mean, I've never seen him drunk, but I think he sometimes has a drink before we get there. I can smell it."

I didn't know whether I was supposed to say something disapproving or supportive, so I just nodded.

Elder Merrill flipped his planner closed. "So, you ready?"

"I'm ready," I said with overstated enthusiasm to compensate for my nervousness.

"How ARE you doing, ma'am?" Elder Merrill said to a passing shopper, a woman in her thirties. We were standing on a busy downtown corner.

"I'm all right," the woman said hesitantly. She slowed her pace slightly but didn't stop.

"Good," my companion said with a smile, keeping up with her. "Well, my name's Elder Merrill, and I'm from the Church of Jesus Christ of Latter-day Saints."

The woman paused. "Oh, hello. I'm Trina."

"Hi, Trina," Elder Merrill went on. "What do you know about the Book of Mormon?"

"Uh, not much." Though Trina had stopped, she still didn't look particularly interested. But that didn't deter Elder Merrill.

"Would you like to know more?"

I watched in amazement as my companion managed to get the woman to not only listen to his pitch but walk away with her own copy of the Book of Mormon with our phone number scribbled inside the cover.

"Well," Merrill said, turning back with a grin, "that's really all there is to it."

"Yeah," I said. "Looks easy enough." It didn't look easy at all, but I was trying to sound positive. Inwardly I was terrified. I wasn't as outgoing as Elder Merrill.

"I mean, you're not going to get everybody," my companion said, "but you never know when you might have planted the seed that will yield fruit later."

"Yeah, I'm sure you're right."

"You ready to try it?"

"Uh, yeah. I guess so," I said, taking a deep breath and clutching a Book of Mormon.

"Okay, then. This guy's yours," Merrill said, nodding toward an approaching man and stepping back to observe.

"Hi, my name is Elder Smith," I said as the man passed. "I'm from the Church…."

But the man kept walking without even acknowledging me.

I turned back to my companion. "How did you do that?"

"Do what?" Merrill said with exaggerated nonchalance.

"That lady," I said.

Merrill smiled. "Go on," he said nudging me toward another approaching man. "Give it another try."

"Excuse me," I said as the man came within earshot. "Can I ask you a question?"

I was caught off guard when he actually stopped. "Yeah, I guess so."

"Uh, have you ever heard of the Book of Mormon?"

"Yeah, sure, but—"

"Would you like to know more?" I blurted, afraid I wouldn't get a chance to ask otherwise.

"Well, yeah," he said tentatively. "But I don't really have time right now."

"Oh, that's okay," I assured him. "Here!" I shoved the book into the man's hands. "Our number's inside if you have any questions."

"Uh, thanks," the man said, accepting the book with a puzzled smile.

"You have a nice day now," I called with a wave as he continued on his way. The man nodded and smiled, and then he was gone.

"I did it!" I said, beaming at my companion. Awkwardly, but I did it.

"Good for you!" Merrill said, offering his fist for a bump.

"Hug?" I asked in my excitement, not stopping to think what that might look like.

"Uh, that's all right," Merrill said, declining.

I lowered my arms, chastened. It had been a stupid thing to say.

"I mean, we just don't, you know, don't want to…."

"Yeah," I said, feeling awkward yet again. I tried to laugh it off. "I've just got a lot of energy."

I was shocked when Elder Merrill reached over and gave me a bear hug. People might have been staring.

"How did that feel?" he asked me.

"Good." I wasn't sure whether he was asking about the book or the hug.

"Feels good?"

"Yeah," I said. Both felt good. Really good.

CHAPTER 6

"I GOTTA say, Elder, that's the best bologna sandwich I've had since I was about six years old," I said as I cleared the lunch dishes from the table.

"Really? I thought it was pretty awesome myself," Merrill said, wiping his mouth with a wadded-up napkin before tossing it toward the plates I was carrying. It bounced off the rim and onto the floor.

I bent over to pick it up. "Yeah, 'cause that's the *only* bologna sandwich I've had since I was six. How do you eat that stuff?"

"Hey, you said you didn't want Lucky Charms!"

"Yeah, well, I may have to reconsider. There was enough mayonnaise on that thing to choke a wildebeest."

"Good thing there aren't any wildebeests around here, then," Merrill said cheerfully, pushing away from the table as I began washing the dishes.

A few minutes later, he returned from the bathroom. "You ready to do some tracting?"

"Now's as good a time as any, I guess," I said. It was only a slightly less frightening prospect to me than the street contacting we'd done that morning, but I knew I'd have to get used to both of them. That was what I came here for.

"Okay, then," Merrill said. "Let's go."

THE NEIGHBORHOOD wasn't a bad one. Not as nice as the one I grew up in, perhaps; the houses were a lot older and smaller, but they were mostly neat and clean. They looked like nice people would live in them, I thought. We had just finished locking our bikes to a stop sign at the corner and were approaching the first home.

"Okay, so I'll go first," Merrill said, pulling a Book of Mormon and a missionary tract out of his backpack. "So you can see how a pro does it." He grinned and rang the doorbell.

A moment later an elderly man, maybe in his sixties, opened the door. "Yes?"

"Hello! I'm Elder Merrill, and this is my companion, Elder Smith."

I nodded and smiled.

"We're from the Church of Jesus Christ of Latter-day Saints," Merrill continued. "We're sharing a message in the neighborhood today."

"You Mormons?" the man asked, wary.

"Yes, sir," Merrill said. "We go by that nickname because of the Book of Mormon." He raised the book where the man could see it. "Have you ever read the Book of Mormon?"

"No, no," the man said, backing away from the door, beginning to close it.

"We'd be happy to leave this copy with you. It's free. There's no obligation."

"Sorry," the man said, "I'm not interested." The door closed.

We looked at each other. Merrill shrugged and smirked. We turned and retreated down the walk.

"Pro, huh?" I teased.

"Well, you can't expect everyone to be ready to hear the gospel," Merrill said. "It's our job to discern those the Lord has prepared."

"Oh, right," I said. Then, after a moment, I added, "Well, I discern that he wasn't one of them." I tried to say it with a straight face but couldn't help laughing.

"Okay, smarty-pants," Merrill said with a laugh. "Let's see if you can do any better."

We reached the second door, and I pushed the doorbell. I turned to my companion. "Did you hear anything? I don't think it works."

"Just knock, then."

I knocked on the screen door. Because it wasn't latched, it banged louder than I had expected. I quickly withdrew my hand, as though I could somehow lessen the sound. I shuffled my feet nervously. We heard nothing.

We were just turning to leave when the door popped open. A tiny, gray-haired woman, at least twenty years older than her grumpy neighbor, stood behind the screen. "Hello, boys," she said in a small, unsteady voice. "Thank you for knocking loudly. I'm nearly deaf and I never hear the bell."

"Hello," I nearly shouted. "I'm Elder Smith. And this is my companion, Elder Merrill."

The woman smiled and nodded but said nothing, so I continued. "We're from the Church of Jesus Christ of Latter-day Saints."

"The church?" the woman said, her smile broadening. "Oh, then do come in." She pushed the screen door outward and stood aside.

I looked at my companion for guidance. Elder Merrill nodded at me to go on and held the door for me. We stepped inside.

"I so enjoy your visits," the woman was saying. "I seldom have guests anymore." She closed the door and turned toward us. "Go on and have a seat in there, and I'll just get some cookies. I'm afraid I can't offer anything to drink other than water. I just gave the last of the milk to the kitty this morning."

"Uh, thanks, but that's really not necessary," I told the woman. I wasn't sure what to make of the situation. Did the woman understand who we were? Should we be accepting cookies from her?

"Oh, it's no bother," the woman said. "I don't eat sweets. I only have them here for guests."

I glanced at Merrill and, getting no signal to the contrary, took a seat on the sofa in the living room. Merrill did likewise.

The woman disappeared into the kitchen.

"I think she thinks we're someone else, Elder," I whispered to my companion.

"Don't worry about it," Elder Merrill whispered back. "Just go with it."

Before I could reply, the woman returned with a tray bearing a plate of cookies and two glasses of water. She walked unsteadily with it.

"Here, let me help you with that," Elder Merrill offered, jumping to his feet to take the tray from her.

"Oh, thank you," the woman said. "I'm afraid I've gotten a little clumsy lately."

Merrill set the tray down on the coffee table between the sofa and the chair where the woman sat. "Thank you again for having us in," he said when he had seated himself. "And it's very nice of you to offer us cookies."

"It's nothing, really," the woman said with a dismissive wave. "I'm just happy to have some company."

"Well, we can't stay long," Merrill continued. "But we'd like to share a brief gospel message with you while we're here. Would that be all right?"

"Why, of course," the woman said with a smile. "That's why you're here, isn't it?"

"Well, yes, I guess it is. Now, as we said, I'm Elder Merrill, and this is Elder Smith. We're from the Church of Jesus Christ of Latter-day Saints."

"Latter-day Saints?" the woman said, more to herself than to us. "Now I'm not sure that's the one I belong to. Is that Saint Christopher's?"

"No, it's not," Merrill confirmed. "We're not from your church, but we'd still like to share the message with you, if we may."

"I guess that would be all right," the woman said. "The Lord doesn't mind, so why should I?" She laughed softly.

"Well, thank you. May I ask your name, Mrs....?"

"Connor. Frances Connor. But everyone calls me Franny."

"Thank you, Mrs. Connor," Elder Merrill said with a smile. "I'm going to let Elder Smith here begin." He turned to me and nodded.

I cleared my throat, adjusted my posture, and launched into the lesson. "Mrs. Connor, I'm sure you know that God is our Heavenly Father and that he loves us."

"Oh yes, of course."

"We are his literal spirit children. He has given us this experience on Earth so we can learn and grow. We can show our love for him through our choices and our obedience to his commandments. Our message today is that Heavenly Father has provided us a way to return to live in his presence."

"Yes, yes," Mrs. Connor said through a beatific smile. "Isn't it wonderful?"

"Central to our Father's plan," I continued, "is Jesus Christ's atonement: his suffering in the Garden of Gethsemane as well as his death on the cross. Through the atonement we can be freed from our sins and develop faith and strength to face our trials. Do you believe that, Mrs. Connor?"

"Oh yes." Mrs. Connor's expression remained unchanged. I wasn't sure if what I was saying was actually registering with the woman; nevertheless, I continued.

"Heavenly Father has given us a way to know what is right. He wants to communicate with us, and he wants us to communicate with him through prayer. Do you pray, Mrs. Connor?"

"Oh yes. I say my prayers every morning," she said with solemn pride. "I used to say them before bed, but so many nights I just fall asleep in this chair now."

I smiled. "Yes, well, that's good." I looked to my companion, still unsure whether this discussion was proceeding as it should. He nodded for me to continue.

For the next twenty minutes I dutifully described the role of prophecy and scripture to Mrs. Connor, all to the same nodding and smiling with which she responded to everything I said.

Finally Elder Merrill interjected, "Mrs. Connor, we'd like to leave with you a volume of scripture you may not have read before. Would that be all right?"

"Oh, well, I have a Bible, but my eyesight isn't so good."

"This isn't the Bible, Mrs. Connor. But we'll leave it with you anyway. Maybe someone can read it to you. And if you want, we can always order a large-print edition and bring it to you later. Okay?"

After a few more pleasantries, we took our leave of Mrs. Connor, but not before Elder Merrill made sure to grab a few more cookies.

When we got outside, I turned to him. "Will you explain to me what just went down in there? I mean, I don't think she even knew we were Mormons, let alone had a clue as to what we were talking about."

"That's okay, Elder. She enjoyed the company. And we taught a lesson and placed a Book of Mormon, didn't we?"

"Are you serious?" I said. "You mean that counts?"

"Sure, it goes into our weekly report to the ZLs."

I shook my head. "Well, I don't think that sweet little old lady is ever going to be baptized. And she sure as heck isn't going to read the Book of Mormon. I think we just wasted our time."

"It's never a waste of time to teach the gospel, Elder," Merrill said. "Besides, I just wanted to give you some real-world practice." He grinned.

"You're kidding, right? Are you telling me that whole little exercise was just meant as a practice run for me?"

Merrill shrugged. "Not entirely. She's a lonely old woman, and she appreciates knowing that people care. You know, sometimes the best way to share the gospel is to actually practice it."

How could I refute that argument? It seemed at odds with our charge to seek only the elect who were ready for baptism, but inside I knew my companion was right.

"And we got some cookies out of the deal," Elder Merrill added, holding up his stash with a grin.

CHAPTER 7

SUNDAY, TO my surprise, turned out to be mostly a day of rest. Not that missionaries were allowed to slack off, exactly, but we didn't have to do any tracting or street contacting, and there were no scheduled teaching appointments. Elder Merrill explained that unless we were bringing investigators to Sunday school or Sacrament Meeting, we generally spent our time interacting with members, either seeking referrals or visiting less-actives to shore up their faith.

On this particular Sunday, we also had a district meeting with the other three companionships who attended the Clackamas Falls First and Second Wards.

"So, Elders and Sisters," Elder Harris said after Elder Schmidt had opened the meeting with a prayer. "First off, I'd like to introduce your district's two newest missionaries, arrived just this week. Sister Tulsa"—he indicated a petite brunette—"is now temporarily assigned to Sister Brown and Sister Olson's area. We have an odd number of sister missionaries until next month's arrivals."

"Hi," Sister Tulsa said with a demure nod.

We all nodded and smiled in return.

"And Elder Smith," Harris continued, pointing to me, "is Elder Merrill's new companion. His first greenie."

"Hi," I said.

"So we may as well start with your area, Elder Smith," Harris said. "How did your first week go?"

Whoa. I wasn't expecting to be put on the spot. "Uh, good, I guess," I said. "We did some tracting and street contacting. And we taught a couple of lessons." Unsure what else to say, I looked to Elder Merrill for support, but he said nothing.

"Any conversions? Any baptisms scheduled?" Harris prodded.

"Not yet."

Harris frowned. "I don't know, Elder Smith. Maybe you're not cut out for this work."

What did that mean? I looked at my companion again; he only smirked.

"Just kidding," Harris said with a crooked half smile.

The room erupted in laughter.

"You guys," I said, shaking my head.

"You should have seen your face, Elder," one of the other elders said.

"Okay, folks," Harris said. "We've had our fun. Now let's get down to business."

MY FIRST Sunday as a missionary also happened to be Fast Sunday, which meant there was a postfast potluck dinner after Sacrament Meeting had concluded. Elder Merrill and I didn't have any investigators in attendance, so we sat at a table with the other missionaries.

"So, where are you from, Sister Tulsa?" I asked my fellow new arrival, who was sitting to my left. She was pretty and had kind eyes. I immediately felt comfortable with her. At least as comfortable as two missionaries who weren't allowed to be alone together were able to feel.

"I'm from Bloomington, Indiana."

"Oh, I've never been to Indiana. Is it nice? I mean, where you live?"

Sister Tulsa shrugged. "It's okay, I guess. I've never lived anywhere else, at least until I came here." She gave a shy smile. "And you?"

"I'm sorry?" I said, unsure of what she was asking.

"Where are you from, silly?" she said with a laugh that caught the attention of several of the other elders at the table.

"Oh," I said, feeling not only stupid but self-conscious under the gaze of Elder Harris, who sat across the table from me. "Idaho Falls."

"Oh," Sister Tulsa said. "That must be nice."

"Yeah," I said. "It's not bad." From the corner of my eye I could see that Elder Merrill, who was on my right, was also listening in on our conversation.

"We should go, Elder," he said. "We need to finish our report for last week and go over this week's schedule."

"Uh, sure," I said, pushing back from the table and standing up. "It was nice talking to you," I said to Sister Tulsa.

Twenty minutes later we were back in the apartment, slipping out of our sweaty Sunday clothes. Elder Merrill had barely spoken to me on the ride home. I had the impression I'd done something to tick him off. Was it something I'd said? Was it because I'd been talking to Sister Tulsa?

In any case, Elder Merrill seemed to have gotten over it by the time we arrived home and sat down for our weekly planning session. "So we got a couple of member referrals today that we can follow up on this week," he said.

"That sounds good," I said. Anything that got us out of tracting sounded good to me.

"We should at least be able to place a couple of BOMs."

"Bombs?"

"Books of Mormon," he said. "B-O-Ms?"

"Oh yeah," I said. "I guess I should have figured that out."

"You'll pick up the lingo soon enough."

I laughed. "I guess I'd better. How long until I'm no longer considered a 'greenie,' anyway?"

"Until there's somebody greener than you."

"Right. Well, I guess somebody has to be low man on the totem pole."

"Yep," he said, turning back to the open planner on the table. "Now, we also have a dinner appointment with an investigator on Thursday."

"Really? Even the nonmembers feed us?"

"It's unusual, but this guy—his name is Jim Davis—is the coworker of the Elders' Quorum President, Dave Benson. I think this could be a good prospect for membership."

"Nice," I said. "Does he have a family?"

"I don't know. Brother Benson didn't say."

"Well, I guess it doesn't matter. I mean, at the MTC they told us finding worthy priesthood holders was our highest priority, right?"

"Yeah. I'd much rather teach men," Elder Merrill said. "They're harder to convert, but they're much more solid converts. Too many missionaries go around baptizing women who are just starved for male attention and not really pure in heart. Or worse, they baptize girls who are crushing on them. A lot of the women who end up getting baptized are single moms, who only become a burden to the church. And the young, single girls usually become inactive as soon as the missionary they had the crush on leaves."

I shook my head. "I don't understand why someone would make such an important decision for such frivolous reasons."

"All right," he said, closing the planner. "I'm going to fill out the weekly report now, and you can watch me. Then you'll be able to do it next week."

"OKAY," ELDER Merrill said when he'd completed the report. "It looks like we're done a little early. We've still got forty-five minutes before lights out. We could either do some joint scripture study or we could just read separately."

"Oh, well, I don't mind… I mean, either one's okay with me," I said, though I didn't really feel like scripture study. I'd eaten two bowls of ice cream and was having a sugar crash. But it felt wrong to just go to sleep early.

"Well, yeah, me too," Merrill agreed. "So, okay, if it doesn't really matter, why don't we just do our own thing?"

"Yeah, great," I said. I got up and started preparing for bed. Elder Merrill did the same.

When I emerged from the bathroom, Elder Merrill was already in bed reading. As I knelt down to pray, I couldn't help but notice the book's title. It was *The Catcher in the Rye*. What was that all about? Missionaries weren't supposed to read secular stuff, except maybe on P-day, which wasn't until tomorrow.

But even on P-days we were supposed to avoid things that might detract from the spirit of the work. I'd never read that book, but I was pretty sure it wasn't conducive to the Spirit. I thought better of asking him about it, though. I didn't want to sound accusatory. Besides, Elder Merrill was my senior companion, so he must know what the rules were.

When I finished my prayers, I opened my eyes and saw my companion was looking at me. When our eyes met, he quickly returned to his book. I watched as he appeared to underline a passage with a Sharpie. I couldn't help myself. "What are you doing?" I asked as I climbed into bed.

"Seeking greater light and knowledge."

"From that?" I asked.

"Well, yeah," he replied. His tone was a little defensive. "If you ignore the bad language, there are some good lessons to be learned here."

"And just how, exactly, does one 'ignore' bad language?" I asked.

He turned the book toward me. "I cross it out."

CHAPTER 8

Dear Mom, Dad, and Mary Anne, I wrote.

> *It's already P-day again! The time goes so fast because we are busy from morning until night, seven days a week.*
>
> *Mission life has been going well, and I think I'm getting into the swing of things. The life of a missionary is very routine. We rise early, then after we pray, Elder Merrill and I go for a run. I'm happy to be able to continue running daily. It feels good to stay in shape, and it invigorates me for the day ahead.*
>
> *After we've had breakfast and washed up, we do our scripture study, first alone and then together. I really enjoy the joint study time. I am learning a lot from Elder Merrill.*
>
> *We are usually out the door by 9:00 a.m. Missionaries will talk about the Gospel anywhere, anytime. We spend most of our day giving lessons, tracting for those interested in the truthfulness of the Book of Mormon, upholding appointments with investigators, and planning for upcoming meetings.*
>
> *Despite being called every name in the book on a daily basis, things are overall going well, and have been smooth thus far.*
>
> *I miss you all and love you all.*
>
> RJ

MISSION LIFE was basically what I had expected it to be, except when it wasn't. I had envisioned a monastic life, where all contact with others would be spiritual in nature, where secular concerns would not intrude. A rigid, dogmatic schedule with no time for personal concerns—except between ten and five on P-days, such as today.

It *was* all those things, in a way, but it surprised me how often the conversations we had with members, investigators, and other missionaries had nothing at all to do with the gospel. It seemed everybody wanted to talk about politics, the news, or just themselves.

And how many times had people asked me about my personal life—my family, my studies, my girlfriend?

"That's the way it's supposed to be," Elder Merrill said when I brought it up one day after our morning scripture study. "People won't take the message to heart until they trust the messenger. And they've got to get to know us to trust us."

"But the truth is the truth," I countered. "The Spirit will confirm it. You know, Moroni 10:4: 'he will manifest the truth of it unto you, by the power of the Holy Ghost.' It shouldn't matter who the messenger is."

"Yes, but a person can't pray about the message to get that confirmation until they've heard the message. And they won't hear it if they're suspicious of the person delivering it," Elder Merrill said, getting animated. "Look, imagine you had never heard of the plan of salvation. Then suppose a Muslim guy knocks on your door and tells you that alcohol defiles your body, the temple of God. Would you pray to find out if that was the truth?"

"No, of course not," I said. "But I also wouldn't start asking him if he had a girlfriend back in Pakistan or wherever, either. I mean, his personal life isn't going to change my decision. It's irrelevant."

"Okay, so let's say he's not a Muslim, he's just a guy you met. If he told you to go pray about his own testimony of a spiritual witness he had, would you do it? I mean, if you had just met him?"

"No, probably not. But that's because I already know what I believe."

"Yes," he said. "And so do the people we talk to. At least they think they know what they believe. But most of them have never questioned it. They've never prayed for a spiritual witness of its truth. To get them to do that, we've got to use persuasion. And you can't persuade someone unless they trust you."

"So you're saying that asking about my family and girlfriend and all that will get them to trust me?" I could see where he was going, but I wasn't quite ready to concede.

"Well, sure," he said, as though it were obvious.

"It's just that I always feel like I have to give the 'right' answer—the one they want to hear," I told him. "Like their whole acceptance of the gospel rides on whether they approve of my personal life."

"It does, in a way," he said. "Matthew 5:16: 'Let your light so shine before men, that they may see your good works, and glorify your Father which is in heaven.' That's why it's so important that we be good examples."

"Well, yeah, *now*," I said, "as missionaries, we have to be. But what about those times before our missions when we weren't such good examples?"

"What's that supposed to mean?"

"I *mean*," I said more emphatically, "some people's questions go digging around in my past, *before* I was a missionary. Sometimes I don't know how to answer them."

Merrill laughed. "Don't be so overdramatic, Elder. I'm sure your past is no worse than mine. We were all mischievous kids once. I wouldn't worry about it." He threw an arm around my shoulder and gave me a squeeze. "Whatever you've done, the Lord must have forgiven you, because you're here now."

I only half heard what he was saying. I couldn't stop thinking about his arm around me. It was the same gesture Rick Johnson had made the night before he gave up and left the MTC. The intimacy of it also recalled a time before my mission that I would rather forget— that I *had to* forget if I was to serve an honorable mission.

"You're right," I said, slipping out of his grasp. "Thanks." I grabbed my backpack off the bed and began stuffing it with pamphlets and Books of Mormon.

Elder Merrill looked at me for a second, as though he was about to say something but had changed his mind. "Okay, then!" he said, getting to his feet. "You ready to go out tracting?"

"Absolutely."

IT WAS Tuesday morning, and we'd been tracting for two hours when I suggested we break for lunch. Despite my junior status, Elder Merrill and I had agreed to alternate responsibility for each day's activities. Today was my day to be in charge of the schedule.

"Okay," he said. "But may I suggest we finish this apartment complex first? There aren't many doors left."

"Yeah, sure. That makes sense," I conceded. "It's just that my stomach's growling something fierce, and it's kinda distracting me from the Spirit."

"Man does not live by bread alone," he said with mock seriousness.

"No," I agreed. "He's got to have some ham and cheese on it!" We both laughed.

"So, where to next?" Elder Merrill asked.

"Right over here," I said, pointing. "Apartment 6."

Elder Merrill knocked. A moment later the door opened to reveal a disheveled man, about ten years older than us, standing in a bathrobe. It looked like he just woke up.

"Hey," the man mumbled, looking first at me, then at Elder Merrill. "You boys selling something?"

"Oh no, sir," Elder Merrill said.

"Then what? Are you Jehovah's Witnesses or something?"

"No, sir," I said. "We're from the Church of Jesus Christ of Latter-day Saints."

"Oh, well, thank you boys for coming by, but I'm not a very religious man."

"Well, maybe we could just leave you a Book of Mormon with some highlighted scriptures for you to read," I said. I pulled a book out of my pack and handed it to him. "And I'll leave you our number so you can get a hold of us if you have any questions."

"Well, that would be all right, I guess," the man said without enthusiasm, accepting the calling card I handed him. "Thank you boys for coming by. Have a nice day." He closed the door.

I looked at Merrill as we turned to walk away. He was grinning wide and giving me a big thumbs-up. "Way to go, Elder. Rack up another BOM."

CHAPTER 9

I WAS happy when Thursday arrived. Not that one day was appreciably different from another—tracting was a part of almost every day but Sunday, along with follow-up visits on inactives and drop-ins on members. But today we had a promising dinner appointment with the Davises, the referral we'd gotten from the Elders' Quorum President. We'd not only get credit for a lesson taught, but we'd get a home-cooked meal as well. It would be a good day all around.

The day began as usual: a lot of unanswered doors and disinterested people. A few taunts and derisive comments from kids and passersby. We did a lot of walking and pedaling. Three housewives said we could come back when the man of the house was home, though it didn't take me long to catch on that this really meant the woman wasn't interested and was too timid to say so. The husband would have no problem telling us to get lost when we made the return visit.

By the time we showed up at the Davises' door that evening, I was ready for some friendly conversation, not to mention the food that would accompany it.

"Hi! I'm Jim," the man said as he showed us in. "You must be Elder Merrill." He extended his hand as he scanned the nametag.

"Yes, sir. Nice to meet you."

"And you are…?" He looked at my tag.

"Elder Smith," I said before he could finish. "Thank you for having us."

"Sure. My pleasure," Jim said. "Come on in." He showed us down the hall to the dining room. "Honey, the missionaries are here," he called into the kitchen as we passed by.

"Dinner's almost ready," she called back. "You boys make yourselves at home. Help yourselves to the lemonade on the sideboard."

I wasn't sure what a sideboard was, but I spotted the pitcher and glasses on a long, narrow table beneath a painting. I set down my backpack on a chair and moved to avail myself of the lemonade.

"You boys do drink lemonade, don't you?" Jim asked with a laugh. "What with all your beverage proscriptions, we couldn't be sure."

"Sure, it's fine," Elder Merrill told him.

"You know," Jim added as I began to pour two glasses, "if it's your health you're concerned about, I'm not sure all that sugar is any healthier for you than a bit of alcohol."

He might have been taunting us, but my companion didn't seem bothered by the comment. He just smiled and said, "You might be right." He took the glass of lemonade I had poured for him. I poured another glass for myself and said nothing. I was probably being a bit too sensitive after the long day of rejections we'd had. Jim seemed like a good guy.

"Nice place," Elder Merrill said to Jim.

"Why, thank you," Jim replied, taking a seat in an overstuffed chair and motioning us toward the couch. "I can't take much credit for it, though. It's mostly Monica's doing. I can barely match my socks in the morning!"

We all laughed.

"I wouldn't mind a place like this when I get married," Merrill said. "Not at all."

"Yeah," I agreed. "It's really nice."

An awkward silence fell, as we'd run out of pleasantries. I continued looking around the room, trying to find something specific to comment on, but my companion beat me to it.

"That's really a monster TV—that's got to be sixty inches, at least."

"Exactly," Jim said. "It's the one thing in this room I got to pick out."

Jim disappeared into the kitchen, and I wandered over to a large rack of DVDs that stood to one side of the screen. One thing was immediately apparent: the Davises had no qualms about watching the R-rated movies that had been forbidden in my parents' home. *Inglourious Basterds*, *No Country for Old Men*, *There Will Be Blood*. I hadn't been allowed to see any of those, although I'd heard friends at school talk about them. There were also some titles on the rack I *had* seen: *Lord of the Rings*, *Toy Story*, *Inception*.

"Yes!" Merrill said with obvious enthusiasm, joining me at the DVD rack. "*Dark Knight*! An awesome movie!"

"That it was," said Jim, emerging from the kitchen with a large roast on a platter. "Best Batman to date."

"Absolutely," Merrill agreed. "I saw it three times before my mission."

I did not share my companion's enthusiasm. I felt ashamed suddenly to be indulging in secular interests, in the home of an investigator, no less. We were there to teach the principles of the Restored Gospel, not discuss our favorite movies. I wanted to change the subject.

My expression must have given me away; Mr. Davis was staring at me funny. "Why so serious?" he said. Apparently this was hilarious, as both he and Elder Merrill started laughing.

I didn't know what was so funny, but they were laughing at me, obviously. "What?" I looked from one to the other.

"Didn't you see the film?" Jim asked.

"No," I said.

"Oh, well, then you wouldn't get it," Jim said as he set the roast down and began to carve it.

CHAPTER 10

WHEN WE'D finished dinner—during which we answered the usual questions about our personal lives—Mrs. Davis cleared away the dishes with the promise of brownies for dessert when she returned. Apparently she wasn't interested in participating in our discussion, so the three of us remained at the table and got down to the purpose of our visit. I started the lesson, then turned it over to my companion at the usual spot.

"So Joseph Smith retired to the forest on a beautiful, clear spring day in the year 1823," Elder Merrill was saying, laying out the story of the prophet's First Vision that every missionary had memorized. Jim was giving him his rapt attention. That was a good sign.

"He knelt down and began to offer the desires of his heart to God," Merrill continued as I looked on reverently at his side. "And all of a sudden he saw a pillar of light directly above his head." Elder Merrill pointed upward, and Jim's gaze followed, as though he expected to see the pillar himself.

Wow. How cool is that? I thought. *The guy is so into the story, it's as though he's experiencing it himself.* Elder Merrill was good. I had to give him that.

"It was brighter than the sun," my companion went on, riding the momentum. "It descended gradually onto him. Then two personages appeared unto him. One pointed to the other and said, 'This is my beloved son. Hear him.' This was the First Vision." Elder Merrill looked at me, then back at Jim. He took a deep breath before continuing. "We know the Book of Mormon is true. Elder Smith and I can tell you in detail how it has changed our lives and the lives of our families. It's brought us closer together, and I know it will do the same for you and your family."

Elder Merrill paused, waiting for a reaction.

Jim pursed his lips. "Can I ask you a specific question?"

"Sure," my companion said, glancing at me. His expression was apprehensive, like he knew what was coming. I had no clue but would soon find out.

"Where does Jesus tell us that we need to be married in a temple, for eternity, to get to the highest level of glory?"

"That's in the Doctrine and Covenants," Elder Merrill said, stiffening. "A compilation of the revelations given to Joseph Smith."

"May I see that scripture, please?"

"Uh, yeah, sure." My companion grabbed his triple combination and turned to the D and C. He handed the book to Jim. "It's in Section 132. Specifically, verse 19."

Jim took the book and read to himself. Elder Merrill and I exchanged nervous glances. We were both apprehensive now; this was not an area of doctrine either of us was accustomed to delving into, even with other Mormons. And certainly not on a first visit with an investigator.

Jim continued to read, obviously well beyond the verse indicated. "Okay, here. Yeah, this is it. Verse 38: 'David received many wives and concubines... as also many of my other servants.' Then in 39: 'David's wives and concubines were given him of me.' And in 40: 'and I gave unto thee, my servant Joseph, an appointment, and restore all things....'" He looked up at us. "Isn't this a revelation on polygamy?"

"No," Elder Merrill said, bristling. "It's on eternal marriage."

Jim raised his eyebrows and continued to stare at us intently. It was clearly a challenge.

"It does state that under certain circumstances," Elder Merrill conceded, shifting uncomfortably in his chair, "plural marriages are allowed." It was the first time I'd seen him thrown off his game. It was unnerving.

"Okay, so under what circumstances did God allow it? Joseph Smith was practicing polygamy well before this revelation."

I looked down at my hands, discouraged and embarrassed. I didn't want to be there. I was glad my companion was doing the talking, but even he was flailing. It was clear this guy had prepared for the discussion; he'd set us up.

"Well, polygamy was only accepted for the purpose of spreading seed, as it states in Jacob," Elder Merrill said, his tone defensive.

"Okay," Jim said, squaring his shoulders, obviously relishing the moment. "Then how many children did Joseph Smith have outside of his marriage to Emma?"

"I don't see how that's important," Elder Merrill said, his voice rising and cracking. He took a sip of water.

"Well, if he was practicing polygamy to spread his seed...."

My companion didn't respond. He'd been cornered and had no answer. I could see the anguish in his face.

"Do you know what they called him?" Jim asked, twisting the knife further.

"I've heard a few names," I offered in a soft voice, trying to assist.

"They called him 'The Glass Looker.' Glass lookers were not uncommon in New York around 1820. They were con men, shysters. They claimed they could find treasure buried by Native Americans. They would look into a stone or glass and peer into a hat and find the imaginary treasure."

"We've all heard that," Elder Merrill mumbled. It seemed to me he might start to cry.

"Well, have you heard this?" Jim went on. "One of his wives was thirteen years old. So, not only was he a polygamist, he was a pedophile."

At that, Elder Merrill grabbed his scriptures off the table and jumped to his feet as I watched, helpless. "It's clear that we've been brought here under false pretenses," he sputtered. "It's also clear that you've done some preparation for our meeting tonight and that you are far more knowledgeable in our scriptures than you have led us to believe. I'm sorry, but I don't think we can go any further," he said as he stuffed the teaching materials into his backpack.

"Nothing I've said is untrue, Elders," Jim said, basking in his victory.

Elder Merrill did not respond. He simply zipped up the pack and made for the door.

"Don't go," Jim called after him, but Elder Merrill kept on.

I smiled meekly at Jim and turned to follow my companion out the door.

It was a silent ride home. Merrill was lost in his own thoughts, humiliated. I felt bad for him but didn't know what to say. Not that I had enjoyed the attack any more than he had. But I hadn't been the one under fire. I figured there would always be anti-Mormons, and no amount of arguing with them would ever change their minds. It would probably tick them off more, I figured, if you were nice to them, because all they really wanted was a fight.

Elder Merrill said nothing as he unlocked the door and we hoisted our bikes up the stairs and into the apartment. He strode silently across the room and began emptying his pockets, loudly dropping—half throwing—items onto the dresser.

"Elder Merrill," I ventured.

My companion's planner slammed onto the dresser.

"Elder Merrill," I said again, with more force.

"Yes," he snapped without looking at me.

"Are you all right?"

"I'm fine." His voice was taut.

"Are you sure?"

"I'll be okay," he barked. Then, in a more plaintive voice, "I just can't believe some of the things that guy was saying." He turned to look at me. His facial muscles were twitching with tension, as though he was fighting tears.

I smiled in sympathy.

"I'm sorry," he said, walking over to the table where I had seated myself. "I'm supposed to be your senior companion. I'm sorry you saw me lose control like that."

"It's okay. You didn't lose control," I said. I wanted to console him. I felt like I should give him a hug. That's what I would have wanted if I were in his shoes. But I wasn't sure that was appropriate. I really cared for Merrill, but we still hadn't known each other that long. I didn't want him getting the wrong idea.

"Why would he invite us to dinner just to ambush us?" he said, pulling up a chair opposite me.

"I'm not sure," I said.

We sat in silence for a moment. He continued to brood. "I wanted some dessert," I said, trying to lighten the atmosphere.

He looked up at me, perplexed. "What?"

"I really wanted some dessert. Those brownies smelled amazing," I said, only half kidding.

He plucked an empty water bottle off the table and chucked it at me.

"*What?*" I said, catching it.

He just scoffed.

"What?" I asked again, taking mock offense. "I've never been so serious."

"I believe you."

"This is my serious face," I deadpanned.

"That *is* your serious face," he echoed, still not smiling.

"I'd love to see your serious face someday."

He just blinked at me.

"Is that it?" I asked, keeping my own expression equally serious. "Is that your serious face?"

He said nothing.

"It's a good serious face," I teased.

At last, he cracked. A smile played at the corners of his mouth for a second, and then he broke into laughter.

I laughed then too. Again, it felt good. It felt even better to see my companion laugh. He really was a sweet guy.

CHAPTER 11

I COULDN'T find Rick. I'd been pacing the halls of the MTC, looking frantically into the dorm rooms with open doors, frustrated further by doors that were locked. No one would help me. They didn't take me seriously. Rick was missing. I had to find him.

I began to run as the panic rose in me. Yet the faster I tried to run, the more crowded the hallways seemed to become. I pushed my way through clusters of missionaries who, it now seemed, appeared with the singular purpose of blocking my advance. Why were they keeping me from Rick?

I kicked and clawed at my blockers, who only laughed at my futile attempt to make contact. I tried to yell at them but couldn't find my voice. I summoned all my strength and finally burst through the doorway my fellow missionaries had been blocking.

And there was Rick! Standing in the community shower, grinning back at me. I gave a shout—"Rick!" All my muscles suddenly convulsed, and a warm flood of relief coursed through my body. Then Rick was gone.

THE ROOM was illuminated only by the streetlight half a block away. Elder Merrill lay in the bed across from mine. He was saying something. I gradually made out the words: "Are you all right, Elder?"

"Uh, what? Yeah. Yeah, I'm okay." I was drenched with sweat: my hair, my face, my neck—they were all soaked. Even the bedsheets.... *Oh dang.* That wasn't sweat. *Oh man.* I hoped my companion hadn't witnessed my dream. What had made him ask if I was all right? Did I actually shout Rick's name out loud? I was mortified to think I might have.

I lay still, drenched in semen and shame. *Please don't ask any questions,* I thought. When Elder Merrill continued to remain silent in the darkness, I slowly got out of bed and tiptoed off to the bathroom. Oh, how I hoped my companion's eyes were closed and he'd gone back to sleep.

After I'd washed up, I returned to my bed and sat on the edge. Should I try to quietly change the sheets? No, I didn't want to call any more attention to what had happened. The sheets would have to wait until P-day. Instead, I pulled the sheets, blanket, and bedspread fully over the length of the bed and lay on top of them, staring at the ceiling. I tried not to think about the implications of the dream, but I couldn't avoid it. I felt guilty. I felt dirty.

"It's okay, Elder" came my companion's voice through the darkness. "It happens."

So he knows! How humiliating! Please, dear Lord, don't let him have heard me shout Rick's name! What would he think?

IT WOULD be my first zone conference, the quarterly gathering of all the missionaries in the Oregon City Zone of the Portland Mission. I wasn't sure what to expect. I knew there would be a lot of motivational talks. And I was looking forward to reconnecting with some of the elders from my MTC district.

The talks would be welcome; I could always use motivation. Despite my determination to be the best missionary I could be, I still wasn't living up to my own expectations. And my companion and I hadn't been turning in the best of numbers during the previous month. We weren't bad for number of doors knocked, which showed we were making the effort, at least, but all the other indicators—lessons taught, challenges, church visits with investigators—were all in the single digits. And "baptisms scheduled" was a big fat zero.

Missionary work was turning out to be harder than I had expected. Being in the Lord's service full-time wasn't all spirituality; it was a lot like a job. I thought it would make *me* more spiritual, at least. But when was that change supposed to happen? I wanted to be a spiritual giant, to live up to the stories of elders who taught and baptized dozens of converts during their missions. Heck, I'd even settle for being as good as Elder Merrill, who I loved and admired as much as any of the missionaries I'd met.

I couldn't help but feel unworthy to be a missionary. I still kind of dreaded tracting, and I sometimes fell asleep during personal prayer and scripture study. And then there was that horrible dream; I couldn't shake it. Those thoughts had no place in the missionary experience. I had to purge them. But how?

By the time I showered and dressed for joint scripture study, I had decided on a course of action. I would talk to President Pierce about the problem during my personal priesthood interview at the zone conference. I was a nervous wreck about it, but I felt sure it was the right thing to do.

Elders Harris and Schmidt arrived to pick us up at nine o'clock. As we were about to walk out of the apartment, the phone rang. My companion went back to answer it.

"Elder Merrill." A pause. "Oh yes. I'm glad you called!" He turned and gave me a thumbs-up. "Sure. We'd love to." He pulled his planner out of his breast pocket. "Yeah, Tuesday looks fine. What time?" Another pause. "No, four would be perfect. All right. We'll see you then. Bye."

Elder Merrill put down the phone and rejoined us at the door. "Good news. We've got another teaching appointment this week."

"Congratulations," Harris and Schmidt said in unison.

"Awesome," I said. "With who?"

"Remember that guy we left a Book of Mormon with about a month ago? The one in the bathrobe with a Southern accent?"

"Oh yeah. That was my first day tracting."

"You're right, it was."

"I remember the guy. He said he wasn't very religious, but he seemed nice anyway."

"Yeah," Merrill agreed. "His name is Rodney. And we have an appointment with him on Tuesday."

ZONE CONFERENCE was a lot more fun than I had expected. Right after the welcome by President Pierce, we had an ice-breaker activity—kind of like speed dating, which I thought was pretty funny. When I got paired with Sister Tulsa for one of the three-minute sessions, I learned she was a sign-language interpreter. That sounded pretty cool. She said she'd teach me some later if we had a chance.

I loved the camaraderie of the conference, the chance to bond with other missionaries, and to learn how to be a better missionary. After the opening activity, we did some role-playing exercises. After lunch the zone leaders explained the new "eight-point teaching program" that had just come down from Salt Lake. It sounded pretty inspired to me; I couldn't wait to try it out when we got back to Clackamas Falls.

When the evening came, we were each paired with someone other than our own companion and sent to a local member's home for a home-cooked dinner. The member family was asked to have at least one nonmember or inactive member at the table so we might have the chance to share gospel principles.

I was paired with Elder Dalton. "So, where are you from?" I asked him as we waited for the Wetzel family to pick us up at the stake center.

"New Mexico," Dalton said. "A little place called Texico."

"Like the gas station?"

"Yeah, but with an *i* instead of an *a*."

"I've never heard of it," I said.

"Nobody has," he said with a laugh. "There are more lizards than people there." As he said this, he brought his right hand to the crook of his left arm and placed it there on a thumb and three fingers, with the middle finger extended so that it looked like an animal on all-fours. He then wiggled the middle finger like a neck and head sniffing around, all the while making a sucking-slurping noise with his tongue.

I don't know why, but I found it hilarious and burst out laughing. It really was pretty funny. Dalton walked the "lizard" up and down his own arm, then made it jump onto my chest, where it continued to run around. I was in hysterics, but I soon became self-conscious and backed off. "Okay, stop!" I begged him. "Enough!"

Dalton relented and stood grinning at me. "We got lots of 'em," he said. "Just like that one."

"Yeah, I bet you do," I said with a laugh. "And from the looks of it, they're pretty dangerous too."

"The meanest," Dalton said with mock seriousness.

THE DINNER proved to be a really positive experience for me—the highlight of the conference, actually. For starters, we had some awesome barbecued chicken, and fresh vegetables the Wetzels had grown themselves. The buttermilk biscuits were killer, and dessert was homemade apple pie—three of them! They gave one to each of us to take back and share with our respective companions. Being a missionary does have its advantages!

The Wetzels had invited their new neighbors—the Kinneys—to join them for dinner. The Kinneys were a married couple in their twenties with a two-year-old daughter, Alicia. After dinner, Dalton and I were invited to talk about the Book of Mormon. Shortly into our presentation, however, it became apparent Alicia was not going to have it. Her crying and wriggling in her mother's lap made it impossible to continue. Mrs. Kinney apologized as she put Alicia onto her blanket on the floor and tried to amuse her with a stuffed animal.

Dalton immediately knelt on the floor next to the little girl. "Do you mind?" he asked Mrs. Kinney.

"Not at all. Be my guest," she said with an amused laugh.

Suddenly Dalton's lizard appeared, slurp-slurping its way around the living room carpet in front of Alicia. The girl immediately stopped crying and sat mesmerized by the antics of the finger creature. Dalton ran it toward her, stopped, then retreated. He did this several more times until a smile spread across Alicia's face and she waved her arms with glee.

"Looks like you've made a friend," Sister Wetzel told Dalton.

"I'm amazed," Mrs. Kinney said. "I'm going to have to learn that trick!"

The gospel-teaching moment was over, but no one seemed to mind. For the rest of our short visit, Dalton entertained Alicia as everyone else looked on. He bounced her on his knee, giving horsey rides. He twirled her in circles until she got dizzy and fell down. But her favorite amusement, by far, was "the lizard," who, Dalton told her, was named "Ferd."

I watched all this with a mixture of admiration and envy. Here was another missionary who was everything I wished I could be: funny, sympathetic, and loved by everybody. One who could not only teach and persuade, but who could also put people at ease and emanate the true love of Christ that the gospel was all about. I wished in that moment that Dalton could be my companion. Maybe I could learn to be like him.

CHAPTER 12

THE NEXT day was a typical Sunday in many ways. In the morning we attended Sacrament Meeting at the local ward, then had missionary-only Sunday school and priesthood meetings. But the afternoon brought the moment I had been dreading: the interview with the mission president.

While we awaited our turn in the office, we sat in pairs and small groups in the chapel and talked softly. I used the time to reconnect with Sister Tulsa, and she began teaching me some sign language.

"That's good," she said after I demonstrated my limited knowledge. "You already know the alphabet."

"Well, most of it," I said, "except I keep forgetting the hard ones, like *x* and *q*."

"That's okay, you don't need those as often as the others," she said with a smile.

She was sweet. She reminded me of Elise in ways, though Sister Tulsa was more outgoing. And she wasn't expecting anything from me in return, least of all marriage, so there was no pressure in being with her.

"So do this," Sister Tulsa said, pointing to herself, then making an *m* sign with her right hand and placing it over her nametag. "I'm a missionary."

I imitated her. "I'm a missionary."

"Good! See, that's not so hard."

"Yeah, but I bet 'the Church of Jesus Christ of Latter-day Saints' is a lot harder!" I said, laughing a little too loud.

Not long after that, Elder Merrill returned to the chapel from President Pierce's office. He gave me a stern look that made me wonder if his interview had gone badly. "It's your turn, Elder," he said.

"Right," I said, getting to my feet. I turned to Sister Tulsa and signed, "Thank you." She signed back, "You're welcome." Then I signed again, speaking the words aloud, "Remember, I'm a missionary."

Sister Tulsa laughed and signed back, "Yes, so am I."

"Elder!" my companion said, impatient.

"Okay, okay," I told him. "I'm going." I pushed through the door into the hallway. I stopped and took a deep breath, then walked to the office door and knocked.

"It's good to see you, Elder Smith," President Pierce said as I seated myself. "How are you enjoying your first month in the mission field?"

"It's pretty awesome," I said. "I mean, I have a great companion. I feel like I'm learning a lot."

"Yes," Pierce agreed. "Elder Merrill is a good man. You're his first trainee, did he tell you that?"

"Yes, sir. He's pretty good at it too."

"I have no doubt that he is," the mission president said. "But I'd like to hear about you, Elder Smith. How are you doing?"

I licked my lips; it was a habit I had when I was nervous. Priesthood interviews always made me nervous. "Good. Good," I said. "I'm getting the hang of it finally." I shifted in my chair.

"I'm glad to hear that, Elder. Are you praying every morning and evening?"

"Yes, sir. Every day."

"And you're having companion prayer as well? It's important for building strong companionships."

"Absolutely."

"How about personal scripture study? Do you take time to really ponder the Savior's teachings?"

"Sure," I said. I'd been reading, anyway. I wasn't sure how much "pondering" I was supposed to be doing.

"That's good, Elder. Those two things—daily prayer and scripture study—will provide you all you need to serve the Lord."

"Yes, sir."

"Can you tell me, Elder Smith," Pierce went on, "what the first law of heaven is?"

"Obedience." I looked down at my hands as I answered, knowing I would have to confess my problem.

The mission president noticed my discomfort. "Are you being obedient to the laws of the gospel and the rules of this mission, Elder?"

I could feel President Pierce leaning into the question, never taking his eyes off me.

"Yes," I said. "Of course." I paused. "Except," I added, looking away again, "well, I'm struggling with one little thing." I glanced up at the president.

"That's fine, Elder. We all struggle," Pierce said. "I'm happy you're being honest about that—with me, with yourself, and with the Lord."

I laughed nervously. "Well, yeah. I mean, I think the Lord already knows about it."

But the mission president wasn't smiling. "That's true, Elder. But he has established confession as a process whereby we can repent and free ourselves from the bonds of sin. Sharing our burdens with our designated priesthood leaders allows us to lighten the load we would otherwise have to bear all alone."

I shifted nervously in my chair and took a deep breath before beginning the confession I'd been rehearsing for hours. "I... I have a small problem with—" I looked down at my shoes before continuing. "—well, with masturbation."

When President Pierce didn't respond, I stole a glance. He was smiling, but wistful, as though he'd been informed of a death in the family. "It may seem small to you, Elder Smith, but that is a serious problem for a missionary. Unchecked it can undermine your confidence, your relationships with others, and your ability to perceive the still, small voice of the Spirit."

I knew all that, of course. But I had hoped for a more sympathetic response. Instead of feeling unburdened, I felt even guiltier. And I hadn't even gotten to the part about the dream about Rick. Maybe it wasn't the time to bring that up after all.

"But I want to assure you," Pierce went on, "that you are not the first, nor will you be the last missionary to struggle with this affliction. Many before you have overcome it through prayer and commitment and have gone on to become worthy servants of the Lord. You can be one of them, Elder. Do you believe that?"

"Yes, sir." I glanced at him and then looked back at my feet. I wanted to be anywhere but there at that moment.

"Look at me, Elder Smith," Pierce coaxed in a gentle voice that was no less disconcerting than if he had been yelling at me.

I looked at him.

"Hold your head high, Elder. For you are a son of God, an Elder of Israel, and you have been set apart for this work. You must never forget that."

"Yes, sir."

"Repeat this to yourself whenever you feel tempted. Call out to the Lord in your heart, and he will assist you when you feel weak. Can you do that?"

"Well, yes, but...." I was reluctant to go into any detail.

"But what, son?"

"Well, it's just that I... it happens during the night, when I'm not fully awake, so—"

"Wait, is that the only time it happens?"

"Well, yeah. I mean, I wouldn't ever... you know... deliberately do it."

President Pierce laughed softly and smiled in a way that I was sure was meant to make me feel better but still felt kinda creepy. "Elder, that's perfectly natural. It's supposed to happen that way, while you sleep. It's what's called a nocturnal emission or a wet dream. Surely you've heard that expression?"

"Of course," I said, totally embarrassed to be talking in those terms with my priesthood leader. "But I have thoughts that I shouldn't have while it's happening." My voiced cracked as I said that. I was losing it; I was afraid I might cry.

"Son, we can't control our dreams. Not directly, anyway. The best we can do is to maintain pure thoughts during our waking hours. If you do that, the Lord will not hold you responsible for your unconscious thoughts."

I said nothing for fear that opening my mouth would breach the dam holding back a flood of tears. I'd been through this already in my premission interviews, and I didn't want to relive the humiliation. A sudden anger came over me, a visceral reaction to the whole string of interviews I'd been through since my first confession on the subject years earlier. I vowed in that moment I was done with the prying, voyeuristic questions. No one had the right to the intimate details of my life. Yet my unintentional anger frightened me. Why was I feeling that way?

"Now, if you want, there is something you might try—with your companion's help—to control those nocturnal behaviors that trouble you so." He looked at me for a response.

"Yeah?" I managed to say thickly.

"Yes. It's something recommended by Elder Mark E. Petersen, an Apostle of the Lord. And some elders have found it a useful tool. It's not required of you, you understand."

I nodded. I didn't really want to go any further, but I had opened the can of worms, and I didn't see any way of avoiding it.

"And it requires that you have a bond of trust with your companion. Do you have that with Elder Merrill?"

"Absolutely." That part was true; no pretense necessary there.

"Good," the mission president said. "Now, here's what you do. When you retire to bed for the evening, find a comfortable position, with your arms away from your midsection. Then have Elder Merrill take one of your neckties and loosely bind one of your arms to the bedframe. Not tight, but enough to keep you from abetting the process if it should begin while you're sleeping."

Fuh-reak! OMG! I could not believe what I was hearing. I wasn't sure what disturbed me more, hearing my mission president say that or the image of Elder Merrill standing over me waiting to tie me up. I could think of no appropriate response. I sat there dumbfounded.

"Well," President Pierce said, perhaps reading the discomfort in my face, "that's something to think about, anyway."

Right. But I didn't want to think about it. In fact, I couldn't push the image from my mind fast enough.

By the time I left the mission president's office, I had promised to keep my thoughts worthy, to seek the Lord's help through prayer, and to not let Satan discourage me. What I had *not* promised was to engage in any bondage rituals with my companion.

CHAPTER 13

AS WE returned to our daily routine on Tuesday morning, I had mixed feelings about the zone conference experience. On the one hand, I already missed the camaraderie and the new friends I'd made there; on the other, I was reinvigorated by the inspirational messages and anxious to get back to the work, where we could begin implementing the new eight-point teaching program we had learned. The interview with President Pierce was, however, something I would just as soon forget.

That afternoon we had a return appointment with Julia Sanborn, a woman only a few years older than us who we'd visited twice already. She was nice enough but noncommittal. We had determined she was probably one of those "missionary fans" who was more interested in the attentions of the elders than in our message. So we had decided to challenge her; either she would accept baptism or we would thank her for her time and move on.

"Now there are three degrees of glory," Elder Merrill said to Ms. Sanborn after we had gotten the initial chatter out of the way and reviewed the previous lesson concepts. "First, the Celestial Kingdom, which is the highest kingdom." He laid an illustrated card on the coffee table to represent it. "The Terrestrial Kingdom, for people who refuse to accept the gospel but still live honorably." Another card. "And the Telestial Kingdom for the sinners." He paused to let the distinctions sink in.

"And even though the Telestial Kingdom is full of murderers and thieves," he continued, "it's still a paradise."

I found it hard not to laugh at my companion's deadpan delivery. It was obvious he was tweaking the poor woman to test her.

"Well, that sounds really nice." That was her response to most anything we'd tell her.

"The idea is to be in the highest kingdom with God," I emphasized.

"All three sound okay."

Elder Merrill tried one more time. "Still, your safest bet is to earn your way into the Celestial Kingdom."

Ms. Sanborn just smiled.

I wasn't sure if she was still with us, but we'd come here to challenge her to baptism, so I went ahead in spite of her silence.

"So, Ms. Sanborn, as you continue to read the Book of Mormon, we think you will find that it is true, as Elder Merrill and I have discovered. We believe that you too deserve to be in the highest of kingdoms with our Heavenly Father.

"We would like to ask you as you continue to find truth in our scriptures—as it seems that you are—would you like to be baptized and join the Church of Jesus Christ of Latter-day Saints?"

"Uh… I'm not sure."

"There's a singles ward," Elder Merrill added. Somehow he managed to do it with a straight face. I avoided looking at him for fear I'd burst out laughing.

Ms. Sanborn remained ambivalent. We wrapped up the lesson with the usual pleasantries but made no further return appointments. To leave the door open, as well as to remind Ms. Sanborn of her own responsibility in the matter, Elder Merrill told her, "Our schedule is kind of busy for the next couple of weeks, but when we see you at church, I'm sure we'll be able to squeeze in another lesson with you." Ms. Sanborn had not been to church once in the three weeks we had been visiting her. Neither of us expected to see her again.

"Well, that was a total waste of time," Elder Merrill said as we donned our helmets and mounted our bikes outside.

"But remember, Elder," I teased, "you told me it's never a waste of time to teach the gospel."

He sighed. "Okay, what can I say? You got me there," he conceded. As we began to roll, he added, "Still, I couldn't believe it when she said, 'Well, they all sound nice'!"

"Well," I said, "that's kind of what Joseph Smith said."

"What do you mean?"

"Joseph said that the reason the veil is there is because if you could see a glimpse of even the least degree of glory, you'd kill yourself to get there."

"I think that's just an urban legend, Elder. Besides, our job is to find 'the Lord's elite,' those who are ready to lead the kingdom. The followers will come later."

"I know that's what they teach us," I told him. "But that's pretty harsh, don't you think? I mean, shouldn't we just look for the 'pure in heart'?"

"But what good does it do to round up the sheep if there's no shepherd to look after them?"

"And what good are a bunch of shepherds without sheep?" I countered.

"That's not the point. You've got to hire teachers before you send kids to school, right?"

"Yeah, I guess you're right," I said.

I HAD been looking forward to that evening's appointment with Rodney. It would be the first lesson with someone we had tracted out together. The guy had seemed nice that day we knocked on his door. Sure, he was disheveled and looked like a total slacker, but he had kind eyes. I always noticed people's eyes.

We arrived at Apartment 6, and Elder Merrill knocked. We waited. No one answered. I checked my watch; we were only three minutes early. I looked at my companion. I was just about to suggest that maybe we'd been stood up when Rodney opened the door.

"Hey there, boys. Come on in," he said, retreating to let us pass. "Would you like something to drink?"

"No, I'm okay," I said.

"You sure about that?"

"Yeah," we answered in unison.

"Have a seat," Rodney said, gesturing to the couch as he sat in a beat-up recliner at the far side of the room. "Sorry about the mess."

"It's fine," Elder Merrill said.

In truth, the place *was* a mess. And it smelled—of mildew, body odor, rotting garbage. I did my best not to react to the odor as we brushed aside a hodge-podge of garbage to make room on the couch. I picked up an empty beer can and gingerly set it on the coffee table.

When I looked up again, Rodney was stabbing and scratching at the coffee table with a large pocketknife. For a moment I feared maybe we'd stumbled into the lair of a psycho killer. I imagined the guy lunging at us with the four-inch blade.

But before I could worry any further, Rodney put down the knife and pulled a baggie out of the side compartment of his recliner. Though I'd never actually seen any before, I was pretty sure the green stuff in the bag was marijuana. My suspicion was confirmed when Rodney began filling a pipe with it. Neither of us spoke as he put a lighter to the pipe and drew a long drag from it. I looked at my companion with apprehension. Maybe we should leave. But Elder Merrill signaled for me to chill.

Rodney exhaled. "Sorry about that. I know that's probably rude of me," he said with downcast eyes, "but I'm pretty nervous. I haven't had guests in my home much lately."

I couldn't help but wonder if the knife had anything to do with that.

"You totally have a medical marijuana card for that, right?" I asked him, indicating the pipe.

"No. No, I don't," Rodney said, unabashed.

"It's fine. We're not the police," Elder Merrill assured him.

"I hope not," Rodney said with a laugh and then added, "Besides, they don't dress as nice as you do."

"That's true," Elder Merrill agreed.

An awkward pause followed as we exchanged uncertain glances.

"Well, thank you for getting back in touch with us," my companion said at last.

"Yeah. I, uh... after you left last time, I took that book that you gave me. I tossed it right there on the table," Rodney said, pointing, "and there it sat for days while I just ignored it. Then a few days later, I was sitting here and I was watching the TV and there was nothing good on. Over a hundred channels, nothing good on the TV at all."

We nodded our agreement with his assessment. I was quickly learning it was always best to agree, even when you didn't. Most people just wanted someone to listen to them, especially people who lived alone, like Rodney, Ms. Sanborn, and that woman Franny who I taught my first lesson to.

"So I picked it up and I started reading," Rodney continued. "And it wasn't too bad. There were some wars in there and a bunch of stuff I didn't understand, so I thought I'd call you boys up and give you the chance to explain it to me. Tell me more about it."

"Sure," Elder Merrill said. "Tell me, do you currently practice a religion?"

"No. Well, I was raised Catholic, but I no longer practice. Don't tell my mama," Rodney said with a shy laugh.

Elder Merrill smiled. "We won't do that." Before continuing, he made a point of looking around the room. "Oh, were you in the military?" he asked, gesturing to a USMC hat on a rack by the door.

"Yes. Yes I was."

"Iraq?" I asked.

"Yes, sir, Iraq."

"Well, you've done your country a great service," Elder Merrill said.

"Thank you." Rodney's gaze darted from Elder Merrill to his own lap and back again.

"Are you still active military?" I asked.

"No, I was honorably discharged."

"Oh," I said. "Were you injured?"

Rodney paused before answering. "Not physically."

"What happened?" I probed.

"Elder, I don't think he wants to talk about it," my companion said, casting a chiding glance in my direction.

"No, it's all right," Rodney said. "I know most of the guys don't like to talk about this stuff, but I don't mind." He paused to compose himself. "I enlisted with… with my brother, Mark. We were stationed in Ash Shura, in Iraq. We had been there for a while. We were getting close, you know, counting down the days before we got to go home. They sent us a new lieutenant. Green as money, fresh out of college. We were just moving from one place to another, you know. Came to a point where we believed we were in a minefield. What they teach you is to turn right around. Step right back into your own footsteps, you know? That way you don't accidentally step somewhere you didn't step before.

"Mark, he was right in front of me as we made our way back. And I don't know what happened. He must've stepped too far to the right or the left or something… suddenly I was all covered in red, you know, covered in blood. I thought *I* had been killed. Then I looked up. I saw what had happened. Really was my own blood.

"The only thing I could think about was, how am I going to tell Mama." Rodney's voice cracked and he paused again to regain his composure. He took a swig of beer and continued. "You boys sure you don't want something?" he said, waving the beer at us before setting it down again.

"No. But thank you," Elder Merrill said.

"Maybe we should just talk about your thing, right?" Rodney said apologetically. "Get out of Iraq. Jesus wasn't there, I can tell you that for sure."

I was fighting back tears as Rodney's story unfolded. Getting a grip, I said, "Jesus is pretty cool." It was a lame response but the only thing I could think of.

"That's what all the kids say, right?" Rodney said with a wistful laugh.

CHAPTER 14

I HAD slept fitfully, my dreams invaded by images of blood and suffering of the kind Rodney had described to us. As I shut off the alarm and lay staring at the ceiling, I wondered how someone like Rodney got through an experience like that—seeing your own brother blown to bits just a few feet away. I shivered to think of it. No wonder the guy was smoking pot. Maybe there was some redeeming value in getting high after all, if it helped you forget.

I shook off the depressing thoughts and sat up on the edge of the bed. Elder Merrill was still asleep. That was odd. Merrill had always been conscientious about our schedule; he was usually the one to prod me to get my butt in gear. Most mornings he would already be doing his stretches by the time my feet hit the floor.

Not today, though. I wondered if I should wake him but decided to leave him be for the moment. I dropped onto my knees to say my morning prayers. By the time I had finished, Merrill still had not stirred, so I went ahead and did my stretches, then moved on to my personal scripture study. But I couldn't concentrate.

Every few minutes I would second-guess myself. Should I wake my companion? Each time the answer was no. I supposed my reason for that was selfish, in a way. It felt good to be the "good" missionary for once. Though I was very fond of Elder Merrill, I still felt inferior to him—spiritually, emotionally, physically. Now I was in the superior position for a change. Merrill was breaking a rule; I was not. It might not be good for Merrill, but it was good for my own self-esteem.

I stared at my companion, sleeping so peacefully. How innocent and angelic he looked! Elder Merrill was beautiful: muscular, smooth skin, full red lips that were so often spread in a winning smile. He was smart, friendly, enthusiastic—usually—and a shining example of what a good Mormon—what a good person—should be.

It occurred to me that Elder Merrill had, in only a matter of weeks, replaced—and in many ways surpassed—Rick Johnson as my personal hero. Heck, Johnson had quit, but Merrill was there in the mission field. He was there for me, even if he didn't realize it.

I was startled from my reverie when I realized my companion's eyes were open and he was staring back at me. I blushed, as though he might have read my thoughts. I cleared my throat. "Good morning."

"Good morning," Merrill mumbled, throwing off the covers and slipping out of bed. He headed straight for the bathroom without further comment.

I blushed again and quickly looked away as I noticed my companion's morning woody straining against the flap of his temple garments. The uninvited sight stirred up painful memories. I pushed the image from my mind and delved back into the Book of Mosiah with renewed determination.

As a result of Elder Merrill's sleep-in, we skipped our joint scripture study. I said nothing about it as we took our usual run and ate our Lucky Charms. I didn't intend to make a big deal of it; everybody was entitled to slack off once in a while. Nobody could be perfect all the time.

Still, that one variation from the usual routine seemed to throw our whole day off. Even without scripture study, we were late getting out of the apartment. We biked across town to an appointment only to find no one at home. Checking his planner, Elder Merrill discovered the appointment was actually for the following Thursday.

I couldn't help but wonder whether the error had been deliberate, given the funk he seemed to be in. Would Elder Merrill do something like that? Still, I wasn't going to say anything.

"Since we're already on this side of town," he said, slipping his planner back into his shirt pocket, "what do you say we drop in on the Zieglers—you know, just see if they need anything?"

The Ziegler family had been baptized by Elder Merrill and his previous companion the month before my arrival. It was customary for missionaries to follow up with recent converts after baptism, but such member visits were usually made in the evening. Daylight hours were supposed to be devoted to street contacting or tracting.

"Sure, whatever," I agreed. "They'd probably like that."

As it turned out, the Zieglers weren't home. "Oh yeah," Merrill said as we mounted our bikes. "I forgot. Sister Ziegler just went back to work this month."

Again I wondered if my companion was intentionally wasting time.

"Well," Merrill said, checking his watch, "we may as well grab lunch here. It's almost noon, and it would take at least an hour to ride home."

When I didn't respond immediately, Merrill added, "My treat. Come on. There's a great little Mexican place the Zieglers took us to once. It's not far from here."

Lunch was good, I had to admit. And it wasn't even expensive. I refused to let my companion pay for it, though, despite the offer.

"Well, since I didn't buy your lunch," Elder Merrill said as we left the restaurant, "how about some ice cream?"

"Thanks," I said, looking for a way to be tactful, "but shouldn't we do some tracting? I mean, it's after one, and we haven't done any work all day."

He stiffened. "I'm sorry. I guess that's my fault," he said with thinly veiled sarcasm as he unlocked our bikes from the curbside rack.

"No, Elder…," I began.

"No," he said curtly. "You're right. Let's go knock on some doors." He slipped on the backpack and flipped his bike around in the street. The neighborhood we'd been working that month, Thornhill, was back across town, not far from our apartment. It would be two o'clock before we got there.

I kept wanting to say something to let my companion know I didn't blame him, but I couldn't find the right words. Instead I followed him in silence. He was just having a bad day, I told myself. Everybody did once in a while.

We'd been pedaling for about twenty minutes when Elder Merrill pulled his bike to a stop at the side of the road. "Oh man," he said, eyeing his front wheel conspicuously. "That sucks."

"What?" I said, pulling to a stop beside him.

"Would you believe it? I got a flat." He pointed to his front rim, separated from the pavement only by the thin strip of rubber tire.

"Huh," I said. "Did that just happen? Or you think it was a slow leak."

"Beats me," he said. "You got the flat-repair kit?"

"No," I said, shaking my head. "Don't you have it? This was your in-charge day."

"Oh yeah…," Merrill said, zipping open his pack and then fumbling around inside. "Man, you know, I don't think I brought it. Of all days to get a flat."

"Well, okay," I said, not letting on that I was losing patience. "Let's start walking, then."

We wheeled our bikes down the avenue in silence, single file, until we reached Hood View Park, where we could travel two abreast on the park's wide pathways. Discouraged by the day's turn of events, we eventually began to reminisce about happier times before our missions. It wasn't long before our nostalgia led the conversation to basketball.

"It's not even the same thing," Elder Merrill argued. "Karl Malone was on the original Dream Team. He's a legend."

"All I'm saying is that Stockton played in an era of better basketball players. He had Larry Bird, Magic Johnson, Michael Jordan."

"Yeah, yeah, yeah, all right. Have you seen Williams play?" he asked.

"Yes."

"Okay, yeah. The guy can jump out of the stadium. He's, like, three inches taller and twice as fast as Stockton."

"What are you talking about? Stockton was known for his quickness. Plus he had eyes in the back of his head—he didn't need to be tall."

As it turned out, we never did knock on any doors that day. By the time we got back to the apartment and Elder Merrill got his tire patched, it was four thirty, and we had a dinner appointment at the bishop's home at six. So we just decided to kill an hour before heading out again.

Elder Merrill continued with his redaction of *The Catcher in the Rye*, while I wrote a letter home.

Dear Mom, Dad, and Mary Anne,

It's not P-day, but Elder Merrill and I have a little extra time before we go to our next appointment, so I thought I'd send a short note.

Things are going really well, and I continue to learn a lot from my companion. He's a really spiritual and dedicated guy, even if he does get discouraged once in a while.

Today it seemed like the devil was working overtime against us. Elder Merrill overslept, so we missed joint scripture study. Then we biked all the way across town to an appointment that fell through. Then my companion got a flat tire and we had to come all the way home to fix it. All we did so far today was eat lunch!

But that's to be expected, I guess. Tomorrow will be better, I'm sure. There's probably somebody out there right now waiting for us to knock on their door; we just have to keep knocking until we find them!

Well, that's about all for now. I miss you all.

Love,

RJ

CHAPTER 15

IF IT weren't for my companion's behavior earlier in the week, I never would have brought it up. But now, as we shared a rare restaurant dinner, I could no longer ignore it.

"You okay?" I asked.

Merrill stopped eating and looked at me. "What?"

"It's just that you seem kind of distracted lately."

"What do you mean?"

I could hear the defensiveness in his voice. "I don't know. Forget it."

"No, no," Merrill insisted. "Go on. I'm curious."

"It just seems like you don't want to be here."

"Why would you say that?" he challenged.

I wished I hadn't brought it up. But now I had to be honest. "I don't know. When I first got here, you were getting up at five thirty in the morning and you were excited about teaching, but...."

"But what?"

"It just seems like you're kind of slacking off a little bit."

Merrill stiffened. "Well, thank you for bringing that to my attention, Elder," he said, his sarcasm evident. "I appreciate your honesty, and you're right. You're right. I'm going to get back on track—"

"Elder, I was just making an observation. I wasn't judging. I just want to make sure you're all right."

After thinking it over for a minute, Merrill said, "It's not something I can explain easily. I'm sorry. It's just, I don't... I don't know. It's just that I've been thinking a lot about that disastrous discussion with Mr. Davis the other night.

"Here is a man who is pretty comfortable with his life and content without any organized religion. We go into his house, twenty years old, with the intention of teaching him to rethink his entire existence."

"Yeah," I said, "but that's what missionaries do. I mean, that's what we've always done."

"Three weeks of training at the MTC doesn't make me qualified for that," Merrill said, getting animated.

"Chris, it's okay to have doubts. Everybody does." It was the first time I'd addressed my companion by his first name. I hadn't meant to, but it slipped out.

"I know. I know it's difficult," he said, taking no notice of my breach of protocol. "And I know it's difficult for you too. I hear you listening to secular music on your headphones."

"Well, yeah," I conceded. "But only on P-day, and not very often."

"And I've seen the way you look at Sister Tulsa," he accused.

"What? No, no, no." He totally had the wrong idea. I definitely did *not* have the hots for Sister Tulsa.

"You can't tell me your testimony isn't being tested," Elder Merrill continued. "All. The. Time." He struck his fist on the table with each of the last three words.

The two men sitting at the diner counter turned toward the sound. I lowered my voice. "Of course it is."

"So how are *you* holding up?" Elder Merrill asked me, his gaze almost pleading for some answer to his own dilemma. It was the first time I had seen cracks in my hero's armor, and it broke my heart.

"I'm okay. I mean, sometimes I want to be at home. Sometimes I want to be at school," I admitted. "But all in all, I like being here."

"I like being here too," he conceded.

"I like being here with you, Chris." I reached out and put my hand on his. It was an instinctive move; he needed some positive reinforcement. "You're a good companion. I care about you."

"Thank you," he whispered.

"Everything is going to be all right." I smiled sympathetically.

"Hey, you two always that friendly?" The voice came from one of the two men on barstools at the counter.

Startled, I pulled my hand back from Chris's.

"Excuse me?" my companion said, turning toward the men.

"I just noticed he was holding your hand there," the guy said. "It's cool with me, you know. I just wanted to know if you're all like that."

Merrill turned back and looked at me, ignoring the heckler. But the man wouldn't let it drop. "You're Mormon, right?"

Still ignoring the taunt, Chris said, "I got this. You ready to go?" He threw some bills on the table and got up to leave. I followed.

As we grabbed our suit jackets off the coat rack, the man continued his harassment. "LDS, Church of Jesus Christ of Latter-day Saints, right? Where you going? Don't leave. Aren't you guys supposed to try and convert me? Right? Give me the lessons?"

Elder Merrill and I left the restaurant without responding. As we walked the half mile or so to our apartment, taking a shortcut through a back alley behind the restaurant, neither of us brought up the verbal abuse we'd just endured. Nor did we revisit our earlier discussion of my companion's motivation.

"So I got a letter from my mom yesterday," Chris said as we walked.

"Oh yeah?"

"She's trying to set me up with this girl back home."

"Do you know her?" I asked.

"Yeah. Known her my whole life." Merrill sighed. "I don't know. Maybe if I just ignore her, she'll get married before I can say 'no, thank you.'" After a pause he added, "You know, they're dropping like flies back home. Maybe you should keep tabs on Elise. She might have found one by now."

"No, I don't know," I began. "It is what it is." I wasn't sure what I felt toward Elise. My ambivalence had only grown since I'd been out in the mission field. "I always said, if it's meant to be, it's meant to be."

"You know, that's what happened to Elder Harris," Chris said.

"What?"

"Last year, when we were companions, his girlfriend sent him a Dear John letter. Basically it said, 'Hey, met somebody else, going to marry him.' That was it."

"Wow. That's tough, man. Guess that explains why he's so uptight."

Just then the rev of an engine interrupted our conversation. Chris turned. "Shoot."

I followed his gaze toward an approaching truck. "What?"

"I think it's those guys from the restaurant," he said, keeping his eyes focused ahead. "Just keep walking."

We ignored the truck as we continued down the alley. But a shout came from its passenger. "Hey! Where y'all headed? Need a ride?" It was the same guy who'd been taunting us back at the diner.

"No, we're okay, thanks," Chris shouted without looking back.

"You know," the man slurred, "you shouldn't be out so late. Unsafe people come out at night."

Neither of us responded. As the truck moved closer, I could hear what sounded like a disagreement between the driver and the passenger. "Hey, hold on," the latter was saying to his friend. He called to us again. "Why don't you get in? We'll take you home. It'll be safer. C'mon," he said, slapping the truck's door. "C'mon, get in."

The truck moved close enough that I could hear the driver reply, "Let's just go, Craig."

But Craig ignored his friend. "You know, it's all right if you guys like to touch each other." When he still failed to get a response, he continued his monologue, alternating between derision and autobiography. "You're from Utah, right? What part? I'm from Utah. Little town called Ferron. You ever heard of it?" I could hear him taking swigs from a bottle in between his declarations. "You know, my father couldn't get a job because of you people." Swig. "Drank himself into oblivion. Y'all take care of your own, don't care about nobody else. Hypocrites!" Another swig. "Faggots!"

That was the last straw for me. For my companion too, apparently, because we both stopped dead in our tracks upon hearing the epithet. I reeled around and glared menacingly at the man, who was almost close enough to take a swing at through the open window.

"Did I make you angry, faggot?"

I removed my jacket and handed it to my companion.

"What are you doing?" Chris asked, incredulous, as I began rolling up my shirtsleeves.

"C'mon, let him go," Craig taunted, jumping out of the truck. "Don't hold him back. Let him go."

I was on him in a second. One well-placed punch to the nose was all it took. Craig lay splayed on the ground, disoriented, nose gushing. I turned and walked calmly back to my companion, took my jacket, and put it back on.

We walked the rest of the way home in silence.

It wasn't until we were back in the apartment that Chris spoke. "You okay?" he asked, watching me nurse my swollen fist.

"Yeah, I'm still a little shaken up," I said, slumping onto the bed.

"I've never seen you angry before," he said, almost in awe.

"Yeah," I said. "I'm usually passive-aggressive."

He laughed. "Well, you probably just sent a guy to the emergency room. Nothing passive about that!"

"I know it's terrible," I said, my guilt surging again.

"Well," he said, taking a seat beside me on the bed. "I hate to say this…"

I turned to look at him.

"…but he deserved it," he finished.

"Yeah, but Mormons aren't supposed to fight," I said, hanging my head in shame.

"Mormons aren't supposed to do a lot of things," he said in a conspiratorial whisper.

A shudder rippled through me. I didn't know why.

"I think we should keep this to ourselves," he said, still in a whisper.

"I agree," I said. I wanted to forget the incident. I was glad my companion felt the same.

"Are you sure you're okay?" Chris asked again, reaching for my injured hand.

"Yeah, I'll be all right," I said, reflexively withdrawing.

"But your hand's all bruised up," he insisted. He got up from the bed and retreated to the kitchen. A moment later he returned with a baggie of ice. "All right. Come here," he said, kneeling at my feet and pulling my arm toward him.

"Ahh…," I protested as he pressed the chilly bag to my painful knuckles. I shuddered, not only at the cold contact of the bag, but at the tenderness my companion was showing me. I wasn't used to that kind of thing from another guy. Why was he being so sweet?

"Sorry," he said, smirking in sympathy.

"That's okay. Thanks." Our eyes met, and for a moment neither of us spoke as he continued to press the ice pack to my hand. I felt compelled to break the silence.

"Did I look cool?" I asked in jest.

"Yeah, actually, pretty cool," he said in mock seriousness. "If anyone's going to look cool fighting a guy while wearing a long-sleeve shirt and red tie, it's—"

"It's going to be me?"

"It's going to be you," he agreed.

An awkward silence fell over us once again as we stared into each other's eyes. I looked away.

"This is really cold," I said, glancing at the ice pack.

"Yeah, it's ice," he said.

"You got it from the freezer," I said, matching his serious tone.

"I did. I got if from the freezer," he said.

We both burst out laughing.

Later that evening, during which we skipped both our reporting and our scripture study, I emerged from the bathroom to find Chris already asleep. As I reached to turn out the light on the nightstand between the beds, I couldn't help but stop and stare into my companion's angelic face. I thought about the kindness he had shown me earlier, and I felt guilty that I'd been critical of him. As I got to my knees to pray, I asked Heavenly Father to help me show more love toward my companion.

CHAPTER 16

TO SAY this was a turning point in our companionship would have been a gross understatement. Something had broken that day, and neither of us seemed able—or willing—to fix it.

During the weeks that followed, our missionary work—when we did it at all—lacked all enthusiasm. Though we never voiced it, I had the distinct feeling neither of us even wanted any teaching appointments. The few we did have were carried out on autopilot, going through the motions, nothing more.

With each passing day, we seemed to find excuses to skip tracting and street contacting, and we spent more and more time on meals and other logistical concerns. When we did travel to members' or investigators' homes, we would take the long way, stop along the route, and otherwise delay having to return to missionary work. One evening we even went to see a movie on our way home from an appointment.

I could hardly believe we were being so disobedient. But I couldn't deny the joy those indiscretions with Chris brought me. The Lord had certainly answered my prayer for greater love toward my companion. Even though we were misbehaving—perhaps because of it, in fact—I felt an even closer bond with Chris than I had earlier. I didn't understand it, but I wouldn't trade the experience for anything, not even if I could be the top-baptizing elder in the mission.

Yet no matter how much I reveled in the bond we shared, it wasn't exactly something I could write home about. Until now, my letters to my parents and Elise had been full of details about my daily missionary work. I'd write about the people we were teaching and talk about the things I was learning from my companion. But how could I explain what I felt for Chris?

I still received weekly letters as well. My parents were full of pride and encouragement, and they asked about our investigators by name. I knew how disappointed they'd be if they could see me breaking rules and slacking off. They wouldn't understand there were other important things to consider. Like the bond between companions. That had to be nurtured too. You had to work as a team. You did what you needed to, to make sure that bond was strong.

One sunny afternoon as we were trying unsuccessfully to do some tracting—now a rare occurrence—we decided to knock off early and go for ice cream. At Chris's suggestion we chose an unfamiliar route down along the railroad tracks. It was forested and beautiful, just a stone's throw from the river, but the rutted, unpaved path proved impossible for our bicycles. It'd take a solid mountain bike with some killer knobbies to ride there. So we were forced to get off and walk.

"So why don't you ever talk about the wrestling thing?" Chris asked me.

"No need," I said with a shrug. "It's just something I do."

"Well, thanks for your help the other night."

"That's okay. I know you'd have done the same thing for me."

We walked on in silence for a while before Chris added, "You're kind of scrawny for a champion, to be perfectly honest."

"Hey," I said, taking mock offense.

"And you talk more about basketball than you do wrestling," Chris went on.

"Well, there isn't a lot to talk about with wrestling."

"I'm sorry I was being such an idiot that night too. I was… I don't know," Chris trailed off.

"You weren't being an idiot," I assured him.

"Well, thanks for listening, anyway."

"No problem. Your feelings were completely valid and totally normal," I said.

Chris stopped and looked at me. "What feelings?" He seemed suddenly defensive.

"Doubt," I said, stopping to look him in the eye. "Confusion."

"So you have those too?" Chris asked.

"Of course."

We continued walking, again falling silent. I was glad Chris didn't ask for details. I was sure my companion's doubt and confusion were nothing like my own. Not nearly as shameful. Doubting the purpose of your mission calling was a far cry from the kind of thoughts I battled.

Once again, Chris stopped and turned to me. "Have you been tempted since you've been here in the mission field?"

"Tempted to do what?" I asked, suddenly apprehensive.

"I don't know, anything. Anything a missionary shouldn't do."

"You mean like go to a movie?" I said with a grin. I was making light of the question, as much to deflect it as to answer it. I didn't want to admit what my real temptations were.

"Well, yeah, there's that," Chris said without laughing. "But, other stuff, you know…."

"Yeah, sure," I said.

Chris didn't respond right away.

I took advantage of the lull to escape the uncomfortable line of questioning. "You'll have to excuse me, Elder. I'm going to use the restroom," I said, nodding toward an opening in the grove of trees beside the river. I stood my bike on its kickstand and headed into the trees.

I'd barely gotten unzipped when I was surprised to hear Chris enter the grove as well.

"Hey," he said, unzipping nearby. "I had to go too."

"Hey." I focused my concentration on the task at hand, trying to ignore Chris's presence. Ever since high school I'd been pee shy. It was all psychological, I knew; I could do it if I could just relax, breathe normally. Soon it was apparent I wasn't the only one who was pee shy; there was no trickle coming from Chris either.

"Guess we both just have a little bit of stage fright, huh?" Chris said at length.

"Probably," I said. It was no use even trying if Chris was going to keep talking to me. "Well, false alarm." I zipped up my pants and turned to go.

"Wait," Chris said as I passed.

I turned. "Yeah?"

"I guess what I'm really trying to get at is…," he began, hesitating.

"Yeah?" I asked again. This was getting awkward. I didn't know why, but beads of sweat began to form on my brow.

"Were you going to kiss me that night?"

I panicked. "What? No!" I wouldn't dare do such a thing. Did my companion know what kind of thoughts I'd been having? Did he know about my past? But how could he?

"I was half-asleep, but I saw you standing right over me."

"I… um," I fumbled. I didn't know what to say. I turned to leave the grove, but Chris grabbed my arm.

"It's okay if you were."

"Elder," I cautioned him, trying to wrestle my arm free. Before I knew what was happening, Chris had backed me up against a tree and stripped me of my backpack. I knew I should fight this; it wasn't right. It was the very thing I had been struggling so hard to forget, to put behind me. I'd worked so hard to get there. I couldn't just throw it all away. I couldn't… I couldn't….

But it was too late. Chris sought the warm recesses of my mouth with his tongue, and I opened wide to welcome him in. Relief and anguish flooded my brain in equal measure, immobilizing me in their ensuing battle for supremacy. I yielded completely to my companion's passion, barely noticing the prickly bark of the tree at my back as Chris loosened my tie and moved downward.

And then the unthinkable. Tears welled in my eyes as my senior companion, my trainer, unzipped my pants and reached inside. *Oh. My. God.* This couldn't be happening. But it was, and I wasn't doing anything to fight it. Despite the horror and guilt I tried to conjure for the occasion, my whole body responded to Chris's attentions and firmly welcomed the smooth wetness of his mouth.

I shivered with a mixture of both physical response and emotion—guilt muddled with ecstasy infused with disbelief. Tears welled in my eyes as Chris caressed my thighs and lifted his hands to meet the gentle, rhythmic action of his mouth, cupping me tenderly to himself.

This was entirely different than the experience back in Hope Grove. This was an act of love—the man I loved, ministering to me physically as well as emotionally, taking me inside as an extension of the bond we shared. The enormity of the moment threatened to overwhelm me. I began to weep openly, even as my climax built. It was, I realized now, a simultaneous physical and emotional climax—spiritual, even.

I yielded myself entirely to the experience, ceding all control to Chris. I threw back my head and choked out a scream of ecstasy through my sobs. It was the most genuine expression of passion I had ever known.

When the moment had receded to but a memory, the sense of overwhelming joy faded also. Guilt and despair quickly oozed into the void, threatening to overcome me. I didn't know if Chris felt the same. Neither of us had spoken a word throughout the entire experience.

Now, with my shirt half off and my pants still unzipped, I dropped spontaneously to my knees and began to pray. Tears continued to flow down my face unabated. But now they had become tears of confusion and anxiety. *How, how*, I begged my Heavenly Father, *could something so wrong feel so right? So good to be held, to be loved, to be touched with so much passion. And yet....* My prayer devolved into gut-wrenching sobs.

Only when the tears had given way to an exhausted numbness did I realize Chris had also been praying nearby. It was evident that he too had been crying, though I had been too lost in my own anguish to hear it. My immediate response was to get up and go comfort my… what, companion? My lover? My soul mate? What did this make us? Besides sinners, of course.

Chris had sensed my gaze and turned toward me. In unison we got to our feet and approached each other. Wordlessly we embraced. Never had I held anybody so tight. I felt as though the spinning of the globe would hurl me into outer darkness if I were to let go of Chris. Nor did Chris make any move to disengage.

I didn't know how long we stood that way, in the heart of the grove, but eventually we composed ourselves and restored our clothing to respectable condition before returning to our bicycles. Neither of us spoke as we made our way back home. It was as though a single word might shatter the fragile scaffolding of love we had constructed for ourselves. I didn't know, or want to know, where we would go from here. But one thing was certain: our bonding process was now complete.

CHAPTER 17

IT WAS as though time had stopped. Life was going on around us, people driving and shopping and working, talking on cell phones, eating in restaurants, doing all the usual things. Chris and I were going through the motions of a typical missionary's day, but it felt as though none of it counted, like it was just a rehearsal for a play whose run was already over.

My emotions were in a curious state of suspension. I felt neither joy nor anguish, only a tingling numbness, as though my whole body had gone to sleep and the circulation was slowly returning. For the rest of the day neither of us mentioned what had happened earlier. When I did try to think about it, it seemed somehow beyond my grasp, like trying to recall a dream after coming fully awake.

I sat on the edge of my bed, wearing only my temple garments, unsure of how to begin my nightly prayers or even if I should. I was still exhausted from pouring out my soul in the grove. I bowed my head but found no words with which to articulate a prayer. It was not only that my sin was so large, but that I wasn't sorry for it. How could I approach my Heavenly Father while I was still basking in the aftermath of my transgression?

Just then Chris emerged from the bathroom, ready for bed. I looked up and watched him approach. Our eyes met. Chris smiled. I smiled back. Chris held out his hand, and I took it. Chris pulled me to my feet and, without hesitation, we fell into a prolonged kiss, less passionate than the one we had shared in the grove but no less meaningful to me. It was confirmation I had not been dreaming. It was both reassuring and terrifying to know Chris's feelings for me were more than a passing indiscretion.

We pulled back and stared into each other's eyes, saying nothing. Tears welled up in my eyes. The joy I had held in suspension—that my guilt had held in suspension—burst loose inside me. The tears began to flow freely.

Chris's eyes were wet too as he lowered me onto my bed and lay down next to me, resting his head on my chest. He moved his hand down to the gap in my garments and traced lightly across the exposed flesh there with his forefinger.

A shiver coursed through me. Chris's tender touch felt so good. Not just sexual arousal, a spontaneous reaction I couldn't control, but something more satisfying, more fulfilling. An affectionate gesture that went much deeper, as though Chris was a missing piece of me that had been restored. He completed me somehow.

I ran my fingers through Chris's beautiful red hair. He reached up, took my hand, and kissed my fingertips, one by one. Neither of us spoke as we reveled in each other's touch. I planted kisses on each of Chris's eyelids. He traced slow lines along the length of my torso, from navel to nipple and back again. We explored each other as though appreciating a newly discovered piece of fine art. An hour or more passed this way.

I could have been content to remain thus engaged indefinitely, but physiology intervened. My erection, as well as Chris's, demanded to be satisfied, and eventually we yielded to them. Slowly, gently at first, Chris slid down my torso and took me into his mouth. I gasped at the accompanying rush of physical pleasure, which in itself was profound. But once again the emotional release was equally intense, and my tears began to flow.

I reached down and stopped Chris, pulling him up beside me and reversing roles. I didn't want the moment to be all about me. I slid down his torso and created for him the same experience he had just given me. Soon he was gasping with sobs. We alternated this exchange until both of us were fully spent and collapsed into an intertwined embrace. I struggled to find words to describe, even to myself, the intensity of the passion I had just experienced, the sense of unity and trust. It was unlike anything I had ever known.

THE NEXT thing I remembered was waking up, still wrapped in Chris's embrace, as broad daylight streamed in through the windows. Chris was already awake, his head on my chest. When I stirred, Chris spoke.

"We're bad Mormons, aren't we?" he said, looking up into my eyes.

"Yeah, I think so," I said reflexively. I didn't want to dwell on that thought for fear it would ruin this beautiful moment.

But Chris continued. "Think we're headed for outer darkness?" he asked, toying with the hair on my chest.

"Uh… I don't know," I said blankly. "What do you think?"

"I think we're a shoo-in," Chris replied with a wistful laugh. After a moment he turned to look me in the eye. "So, RJ," he said, lingering on my name as though rolling a fine wine over his tongue, "you ever been with girls?"

"No, not really."

"What about What's-Her-Name?"

"Well, we came close, but no. The first time I ever kissed a girl, I set myself up for failure, because I prayed and prepared myself to like it, and then when it happened—I mean—it was just a kiss, that's it. You know, nothing else."

"That's when you knew?" Chris asked.

I didn't answer right away. I had to think about that. When did I really know? I'd never had to answer that question before. I'd never discussed this with anyone before. At length I answered. "I always knew how I felt, but… well, there's a place near my home called Hope Grove. It sits on a bank near the falls in Freeman Park, and I didn't know what it was used for.

"One morning, I woke up really early and I couldn't fall back to sleep, so I got up to go shoot hoops. While there, I started to hear something in the bushes. I looked around to see where the noise was coming from, but I couldn't see anything. So I walked toward it. And I saw two men. One was on his knees, and the other was pinned up against a tree. And I just stood there and watched. One of the guys noticed me and smiled, so I walked closer.

"I had been affectionate with men before, but that… that was very different," I said. I suddenly felt maybe I'd gone into too much detail. I didn't want Chris to think I was promiscuous. "But that was the only time," I added. "Anyway, I'm feeling a little long-winded."

"No, that's okay. I like it when you talk," Chris said. "I get the feeling you don't often get the chance to."

It was sweet to hear Chris say that. I'd always been on the quiet side; I didn't generally go into a lot of detail. And this was definitely a subject I'd never discussed with anyone, so it felt good to talk about it, even though I'd always been ashamed of the experience. I hadn't meant to bring it up, but I had such a complete trust in Chris, it just kind of came out.

"What about you?" I asked. "When did you know?"

"I remember I went out to eat with my family," Chris said. "I was about nine years old. At the restaurant I was sitting next to my dad when, a few tables down, I saw this really good-looking boy about my age. So I said in front of my mom and dad and brother and sister, 'Hey, that's a really handsome boy.'

"They completely ignored me at the time, but when we got home, my dad pulled me aside and yelled at me. He told me I shouldn't think things like that and I should never say something like that ever again.

"There's always been a rift between me and my dad because I think he's always known—"

Chris's story was interrupted by a knock at the door. We looked at each other momentarily, frozen in panic. Then, in unison, we flew out of bed and began to put our pants on. Another knock.

"Just a minute," I called as I finished dressing. Still disheveled, I opened the door to find Elder Harris. "Hey."

"Hey," Harris said, walking past me into the apartment. "What took you guys so long to answer?"

"We were just reading some scriptures, and we were really into it today," I lied.

"Yeah," Chris added.

"Really?" Harris asked, doubtful. "What uh, what verse?" he challenged.

"First Nephi 2:15," Chris said without hesitation.

I stifled a laugh and wondered if Harris would get the joke. The verse in question, the shortest in the Book of Mormon, said nothing more than "And my father dwelt in a tent."

Apparently Harris was clueless. He thought for a second before replying, "That's a good one. So what are you guys up to?" he asked, looking around.

"Just studying, like we said," I reiterated.

"Yeah, well, uh, let's go shoot some hoops," Harris said.

"Actually, I don't feel like playing any basketball right now," Chris said.

"Well, I really want to go, and it's P-day. You don't have any appointments, so—" He looked from Chris to me and back again. "—let's go shoot some hoops."

"Yeah, okay," I conceded. "We'll be out in a minute." I was just anxious to get the zone leader out of the room so Chris and I could catch our breath and recover from the adrenaline rush.

When we finally got Elder Harris out the door, we both sighed with relief. I rolled my eyes at Chris. "Man, that was close!"

Twenty minutes later we were at the park, playing H-O-R-S-E. I took a shot and missed. "Dang it!"

"So what have you guys been up to?" Elder Harris asked out of the blue.

Was he on to us? Why else would he ask? He knew what missionaries did each and every day. He was probing. "Nothing much," I said, stealing a glance at Chris. "Just some tracting, challenging, the usual."

"Well, your numbers are low. The lowest in the zone, in fact," Harris said, passing the ball to my companion. "What's been going on?"

Chris looked at me.

"What are you looking at him for?" Harris said with derision. "You're the senior here. I'm talking to you, Elder Merrill. We haven't seen you guys in church," he scolded. "You haven't been calling in your numbers. It's been like pulling teeth to get them from you."

"We've been sick," Chris said.

"You've both been sick?" Harris's tone challenged Chris's claim.

"Yeah," I interjected, backing up my companion's lie. "I was sick and then I gave it to Elder Merrill." *And maybe it wasn't a lie after all*, I thought cynically. Church leaders considered guys like us to be "sick," didn't they?

"Really?" Harris said, his sarcasm unmistakable.

"Yeah," Chris said, defiant.

Realizing he couldn't prove his suspicion, Harris countered, "Well, you should have said something. The bishop and mission president were getting concerned. I'll let them know."

Harris took a shot. I jumped in and grabbed the rebound. I took a shot of my own and missed. Chris caught the rebound. Elder Harris, who had retired to the sideline to take a swig from his water bottle, looked at me. "You're a whore, by the way."

I was taken aback. Even for the prickly zone leader, this was out of character. "What?" A moment of panic swept over me; did Harris know what had been going on? But how could he?

"Oh," Harris answered offhandedly. "You had an *H*, an *O*, and that was an *R*."

I sighed with relief and stole a look at Chris.

"Whore," he whispered, passing me the ball with a wink and a barely concealed smile.

CHAPTER 18

THE CLOSE call with Elder Harris, and the suspicions he expressed, had a chilling effect on the momentary bliss we felt during the initial days of our budding romance. We both knew we were marked men; the fragile world of love and exploration—of ourselves and each other—couldn't go on, and we both knew it. Heck, even if we weren't discovered, Chris only had three more months remaining in his mission.

Either way, I knew there was no going back at that point. We had leaped over the precipice together, like Thelma and Louise, and the ground was rising swiftly to meet us; it was inevitable. I figured we might as well enjoy the view on the way down.

We hadn't discussed it outright, but it seemed Chris had reached the same conclusion. As we rode the train to Rodney's one afternoon later in the week, Chris suddenly leaned over and gave me a kiss on the cheek, then straightened my tie. I smiled back at him, but I couldn't help but wonder what other passengers might be thinking. Almost everybody recognized a couple of Mormon missionaries when they saw us. But I was pretty sure no one had ever seen two of us kiss in public.

We weren't exactly being the shining examples of our faith we had been sent there to be. Yet even as I thought that, I felt a surge of indignation. Chris and I were still Mormons, and we were still missionaries. Why should our experience be hidden so we could imitate somebody else's instead? We were being real, being honest. We loved each other. Why should there be any shame in that?

Still, I could imagine what church members would think if they saw us. Or my friends and family. I knew what the other missionaries would think. I'd heard antigay slurs back at the MTC, and even one at the recent zone conference. It had bothered me, but mostly because it had made me feel guilty. Strangely, however, I didn't seem to care what they thought now. All that mattered in this moment was being with Chris. With Chris by my side, I could weather whatever lay ahead. I turned to look at him. Chris returned the look and smiled. That was enough.

"How you boys doing? It's been a while," Rodney said after he answered our knock, closed the door, and made for the recliner in which he appeared to spend most of his waking hours.

"Yeah," I agreed, taking a seat on the sofa. Chris did likewise. I couldn't help but reflect on how much had changed since the last time the three of us occupied those same seats.

"How you been?" Rodney asked.

"Really, really good." Even as I said it, I was surprised at myself. By most standards, the recent turn of events was anything but good for a Mormon missionary. Yet I did feel good. There was something inside me I couldn't readily define, but it was good, and Chris was most definitely at the center of it.

"Good. All right," Rodney said, settling into his chair. "All right, I'm surprised I haven't heard from you more. I thought you boys were supposed to be hounding me, trying to convert me and baptize me or something." His tone was not accusatory.

"Well, we're just glad you called," I said.

"Yeah," Chris agreed.

I wasn't sure what Rodney expected of us, nor did he seem sure what we were prepared to offer him. Officially, of course, we were representing the church and the Restored Gospel. But could we really?

"Yeah, well," Rodney said, reaching for the Book of Mormon that lay on the coffee table before him. "I've been reading some of those scriptures you highlighted for me in the book."

"Good, good," I said. It was a perfunctory response. It really didn't matter to me now whether Rodney read the Book of Mormon. It wasn't about that anymore. I didn't want to preach about being a Christian; I just wanted to get on with living a Christlike life. That's what was really at stake. Being Rodney's friend was the first priority.

Rodney put the book down. "You boys mind?" he asked, opening the armrest of the chair and reaching into the compartment beneath it. "I know you're probably not supposed to be around this stuff." He waved a baggie of green herb.

"No, go ahead," Chris encouraged.

"Sure," I agreed.

Rodney smiled. As we looked on, he packed the pipe, lit it, and took a hit. He held it in for an incredibly long time. When he finally did exhale, he remained motionless, as though lost in thought.

"Rodney?" Chris probed after a prolonged wait.

"Rodney," I said with more force when he didn't respond.

Rodney came around. "Yeah? Oh right, the scriptures. Um… yeah, I," he began. "I…." He started again. "The scriptures that you highlighted for me in yellow were very pretty, but a bit repetitive."

"Yeah," Chris agreed.

Rodney tried again. "And, uh…."

I jumped in to help him. "And it came to pass, and it came to pass…."

"Yeah, yeah, yeah," Rodney said, suddenly animated. "Says the same thing over and over and over." He thought for a minute. "You know, Mark Twain said the Book of Mormon was 'a prosy detail of imaginary history, and a tedious plagiarism of the New Testament.'"

"Well, I don't think Mark Twain had anything positive to say about any organized religion," Chris countered. He turned to me. "What do you think?"

"I would agree," I said.

"Yeah, I suppose you're right about that," Rodney conceded.

"Where are you getting your information, by the way?" I asked. I wasn't so much offended as curious how this war-weary shut-in suddenly became versed in Mark Twain and the Book of Mormon.

"Mostly from the Internet," Rodney said.

Conversation faltered for a moment, each of us lost in his own thoughts.

"Hey, can I see that?" I said, reaching for the baggie. It was an entirely impulsive request.

Rodney, misunderstanding, began to hand me the Book of Mormon. "You gave it to me."

"Oh no," I clarified. "The bag of… the green."

Rodney handed me the pot.

I held the open bag under my nose and took a deep whiff. "It smells really good." I stretched it toward Chris. "Here." But Chris waved me off.

"Yep," Rodney said proudly, as though the scent were his doing. "That's one of the best things about it."

"Could I see the…," I began, reaching for the pipe.

"The pipe? Yeah, go for it. No problem," Rodney replied, handing over the small glass pipe into which he had packed the marijuana.

"RJ, what are you doing?" Chris asked, incredulous.

"I just want…." But I didn't know exactly what I wanted. I just felt free suddenly, to make a decision for myself. One that wasn't prescribed for me. "I think I'm going to try it."

"Why?" Chris was perplexed but not accusatory.

"I'm just kind of curious to see what…." But again I failed to articulate a reason. I didn't really know why; maybe I felt I could just throw caution to the wind because I was already condemned. "Is there some in there?" I asked Rodney.

"Yeah, it's already packed."

I held up the pipe. "I saw you do this once," I told him, tapping the pipe a couple of times. "So I'll do that too."

Rodney laughed.

"Okay, so…," I said, unsure of how to proceed but now fully committed to the venture.

Rodney jumped in to help. "All right, well, you're going to want to hold the side there. You see that little hole? That's called the carb."

I found it with my finger and pressed.

"You want to hold on to that, and it creates pressure in the glass. And then you put it up to your mouth, you light it, you suck in, and then you let go of the carb. And it all rushes in."

"Okay," I said, putting the pipe to my lips and raising the lighter. I still wasn't quite sure what I was doing.

"I can guide you through it," Rodney encouraged. "Just go ahead and start." Rodney did a drumroll on the table.

I took a draw on the pipe. I knew I was doing it right because it burned going down my throat. I felt tears welling in my eyes. When I could hold the smoke in no longer, I blew it out. I struggled for a moment, trying to catch my breath. When I finally did, I threw my head back and laughed. I couldn't believe I had done it. I rolled my eyes in amazement at my own audacity.

When I looked up again, Rodney and Chris were staring at me expectantly. "You guys," I said, suddenly self-conscious. Then to Rodney I said, "What's it supposed to make you feel like? I've never done this before."

"You've never done any weed before?" Rodney asked.

"I'm Mormon," I said. What more explanation was needed?

"He *is* Mormon," Chris added, as though Rodney might have doubted the correlation.

"It's just gonna make you feel...." Rodney hesitated. "Interesting." He turned to Chris. "Chris, you can feel free if you'd like. No pressure."

I extended the pipe to my companion. "Do you wanna?" I didn't really expect him to do it—he was the son of a General Authority, after all. But then again, maybe that reasoning was moot, given the nature of our relationship.

Chris hesitated. "All right," he said at last. He took the pipe and put it to his lips; then he sucked at it tentatively.

"You got it?" I asked.

Chris pulled the pipe away from his mouth and laid it on the table. "I don't feel anything," he said after only a few seconds. He looked from me to Rodney.

"Well, maybe you just didn't do enough, or didn't do it right," Rodney said. "Besides, it usually takes a while."

CHAPTER 19

TWENTY MINUTES later—or was it longer than that? I couldn't be sure—I was definitely feeling the effects. I'd never been high before, or even drunk, so I had nothing to compare it to. It was like everything was in really sharp focus. Well, everything I focused on, anyway. Stuff on the periphery was kind of blurry. Not literally blurry but like it was far away. That wasn't really right either. I thought about how to describe it.

"RJ?" Somebody somewhere said my name. "RJ!" Chris was speaking loudly in my ear. I turned to look at him. I was still in the same place, on Rodney's couch. How long had I been there?

"Hi," I said. I was happy to see Chris.

"You okay?" my companion asked.

"Sure, yeah?" I said, feeling kind of dreamy. "How are you?"

"Well, I'm certainly not feeling as good as you seem to be," Chris said with a laugh. He stared intently at me. His blue eyes were even more beautiful than I remembered.

"Is this normal?" Chris asked. He was talking to Rodney now. I had almost forgotten Rodney.

"Hi, Rodney," I said. "How are you?"

Rodney laughed. "I'm fine, RJ. And I'm guessing you're fine too." To Chris he said, "Yeah, don't worry about RJ. He's right where he needs to be." After a moment he asked, "You boys allowed to watch TV?"

I looked at Chris, who returned the look. How silly a question it seemed after what we'd been doing all week. And now we were smoking pot! What difference would it make if we watched TV?

"Not really," Chris said. "I mean, I haven't watched TV in a long time." After a pause he added, looking to me, "But I suppose a little...."

"Yeah," I agreed. "I wouldn't even know what's on anymore."

Chris said with more conviction, "A little bit wouldn't hurt."

"Well," Rodney said, "do you want to watch a movie?"

"Yeah, sure," Chris and I answered in unison.

"I've got *Finding Nemo* and *Princess Bride*." Rodney paused.

"Yeah, those are good," Chris said, turning to me for a confirmation.

"*Saving Private Ryan*?" Rodney went on.

"Those are okay," I said. I was feeling good now and didn't really care what we watched.

"Would you want to watch those?" Chris asked Rodney.

"*Full Metal Jacket*?" Rodney continued.

"You got increasingly violent, I see," I told him.

"Those sound like war movies," Chris said. "I mean, are you okay to watch those?"

"Well, sometimes I watch them," Rodney said with a shrug. "*Sex and the City*?"

"*Sex and the City*?" I asked. I'd heard of that. I wasn't sure what it was about, but it seemed an odd choice for Rodney. Definitely not in the same category as the other movies he suggested.

"Yeah, yeah, it's about girls in New York," Rodney said. "They run around and have sex with everybody."

"Oh," Chris said. "Is that the show about the three hookers and their mom?"

"You're talking about *All in the Family*," I corrected him.

"No," Rodney said. "That's *Golden Girls*."

Rodney said something else, but I missed it. I was suddenly aware of how ravenously hungry I was. How long had it been since breakfast?

"Yeah, it's nice," I heard Chris say.

"Do you have any snacks?" I asked, suddenly starving.

Chris turned to me. "No, we're talking about his knife."

My head was buzzing, and I felt like all my senses had been juiced with electricity. "Oh. Woo!" I stretched my arms up over my head, amazed at how long they seemed to be. Had they always been that long? My hands came to rest on a tapestry hanging above the couch. "This is nice," I said, craning my neck to admire it. "Has this been here the whole time?"

"Yeah," Rodney said. "It's been there ever since I moved in, in fact. I don't even know what the heck it's supposed to be."

"You guys remember raising the roof?" I asked. I moved my extended palms up and down toward the ceiling, demonstrating the dance move. "That was pretty cool," I added. I was still marveling at how long my arms were.

"I have no idea what you're talking about," Rodney said without any inflection whatsoever. "Hey, you fellas wanna order some tacos? I know a place up the street that delivers."

"Yes!" I said. "I could eat a dozen of 'em right now. I'm starved!"

"Sure," Chris said. "I could eat a few myself."

"All right, then." Rodney grabbed the phone and placed the order. When he was done, he turned to the DVD player and slipped a disc into it.

I didn't know how long it took before our food arrived. It felt like hours. I was into my fourth or fifth taco when a realization struck me. "Chris and I have never seen movies like this with the inappropriate parts in them," I told Rodney.

"Really?" Rodney asked.

"Mormons watch a lot of edited videos," Chris said.

"What?" Rodney asked, incredulous. "You mean the Mormons just cut the violence right out of it?"

"Yeah," I said. "And the sex. The version of *Goodfellas* I saw before this was only about thirty-five minutes long."

"Well, if this is too traumatic for you, we could put on something else," Rodney offered.

"No, no, that's fine," Chris said. He looked at me.

"I'm totally good," I said, stuffing my tie into my mouth. I didn't know why; it just seemed like something to do.

Chris shook his head with a wry smile. "You have a mouthful of tie, sir," he said.

I didn't remember anything that happened after that until sometime after we got home.

THAT NIGHT, as Chris and I lay in bed together naked, I buried my face in his neck. I loved the way he smelled. It gave me a higher feeling than Rodney's weed would ever give me.

We lay quiet for a long while before Chris broke the silence. "So...," he began, but he hesitated to complete the thought. He stroked my hair with one hand; with the other he held my hand to his bare chest. "How are you feeling about everything?" he articulated at last.

I didn't open my eyes; I didn't want to interrupt the moment. "What do you mean, 'everything'?" I asked, stroking the cute little tuft of hair on his chest.

He gave a cynical laugh. "Well... you, me, the mission in general?"

"I guess I'm still trying to make sense of it all," I said. "What about you? How do you feel?"

Chris thought for a moment. "I am not an apostate," he said. The defiance in his voice made me open my eyes and look at him. "And I still have a deep love for Jesus Christ," he continued.

"So do I," I assured him after a moment's thought. I wasn't sure of anything, really, but I wanted to be a rock for Chris. It wasn't the time to talk about doubts.

Chris turned and smiled at me and stroked my hair again. Then he looked away and his smile faded. "But I do feel guilty. I mean, I have to, you know?" He looked back at me.

"Of course," I agreed. "I feel guilty too. How can we not? But, you know, the church doesn't really give us a way to cope with what we're going through. We've got to find a way through this on our own."

"And that doesn't scare you?"

I raised my head and looked him in the eye. "It terrifies me. But this is who we are, Chris. We don't get to choose. I think we're both on the brink of something new, and it's going to be rough, but we'll make it." I reached up and put my hand to Chris's cheek. "Everything is going to be fine. Okay?"

Chris turned and nodded his agreement. I slipped my hand behind his neck and pulled his mouth toward mine. We kissed. And then we kissed again, longer, deeper, and more passionately. When we were done, no more words were necessary. I returned my head to Chris's shoulder and nuzzled his neck. Soon I was asleep.

CHAPTER 20

AS THE weeks went on, we started spending a lot of time with Rodney. We did less and less tracting, until we abandoned it altogether. Now we were about to skip church meetings for the first time. I didn't feel particularly guilty about that, but telling a lie about it was more difficult. I hadn't had much experience with lying; I was never good at it.

"So are you going to call?" I asked as we lay in bed, basking in the morning sun.

"Yeah, but I want to wait until priesthood meeting starts, so I can be sure they won't answer." He looked at the clock. "That won't be for another hour." He planted a kiss on my head. "What do you want to do until then?"

I rolled off him and onto my back. "I don't know," I said, looking at the ceiling. "We could go for a run." Then I remembered it was Sunday. "Oh, wait. I guess not." We couldn't be seen running on the Sabbath; that would be too obvious. I thought for a minute. "We could write in our journals."

"We could," Chris said in a doubtful tone.

"Why?" I asked, looking over at him. "What did you have in mind?"

Chris responded with a coy smile as he reached over and placed a finger on my chin, then slowly traced it down my bare torso. He paused at my navel and made a circle before continuing.

"Again?" I asked, grabbing his wrist and halting his downward progress.

He grinned as he struggled to free his arm. "What, you mean you're not up for it?" Before I knew it, Chris had flipped over and was astride me. "'Cause I think I can help with that."

I wasted no time in pulling a reversal; I straddled him, pinning both his arms to the mattress. "You should know better than that by now," I teased. "I keep telling you, I'm a champion."

"Maybe I just like to see your moves," Chris said.

"Well, I've got a few more," I said, playing along. "Would you like to see those too?"

"Only if they're the stuff of champions."

"Oh, absolutely."

Playfulness quickly became passion as we explored our long-repressed sexual desires yet again. It was as though we were making up for years of pent-up passion and longing. Chris became pliant, yielding to me, allowing me access to his deepest physical and emotional realms. I reciprocated, granting him a look into my own body and soul.

Thirty minutes later sleep threatened to overtake me as we both lay exhausted amid the twisted sheets. I glanced over at Chris, whose eyes were already closed. I stroked his arm. "Hey, you'd better make that call now."

As we'd hoped, it went to voice mail. "Good morning, Elder Harris. This is Elder Merrill. Unfortunately it doesn't look like we'll be making it to church this morning. We were on our way, but Elder Smith just hit that killer sewer grate down at Third and River and banged up his bike pretty good. He's okay, but he's kind of a mess at the moment." Chris looked me up and down and winked as he said this.

I scrunched myself into a crash-victim pose and made a grotesque face at him. When a laugh burst from him, I began writhing on the bed and pawing at him comically.

Chris waved me away and mouthed "Stop!" He slipped out of bed to avoid my advance and continued apologetically into the phone, "Sorry, it's not really that funny, I know. It's just that, well, Elder Smith, did look rather comical for a minute. Anyway, we've got to head back now and get him cleaned up. By then it'll be too late to get back for the meetings. Besides, we've got a lunch appointment with our investigator, Rodney, so we'll catch up with you later."

"You made that sound so easy," I said when he ended the call.

Chris gave a cynical laugh. "Yeah, well, when your dad's a GA, you learn to make some creative excuses."

An hour later, after we'd shared a long, hot shower, we dressed and hit the street. Since Rodney didn't typically get up before one o'clock, and it was still only ten thirty, we had plenty of time to walk.

"Do you think they'll transfer you again before you go home?" I asked as we crossed through the park. The possibility had been nagging at me for days, but I hadn't wanted to confront it.

"I don't know," Chris said, kicking at a fallen branch in the path. "With only two months left, it hardly seems worth it. But then, I've been in Clackamas Falls for five months already, and seven months in one area is a long time."

Neither of us said anything for several minutes as we contemplated what a transfer would mean for our relationship. Finally I said, "I don't know if I could keep doing this without you."

"What do you mean?" Chris said, turning to me. "Sure you can. I mean, I doubt your next comp would let you smoke pot with Rodney, but the rest of it's just the usual routine. The time goes by quickly."

"Maybe it's easier for you," I said, feeling defensive. "Two months might go by quickly, but I've got most of two whole years ahead of me." I forced my voice to remain even, despite my emotions. "Chris, this… this thing… whatever it is we have here… it's changed me. I'm not the same person I was when I got here two months ago."

"Neither am I, RJ," Chris said. "But we just go on. We do what we have to do to make things work."

I stopped walking. "I love you, Chris." My voice broke as I said it, in spite of my best efforts to stay in control.

Chris turned back to me. He hesitated a moment before walking over and embracing me, but only briefly. "I love you too," he whispered, looking around to see if anyone was watching. "I love you too."

As we sat together on the sofa digging into our burritos, Rodney asked, "So, what are you guys going to do after you get home?"

It was a question I had been wrestling with since our recent turning point. Clearly, my future was far less certain than it had been a couple of months earlier, when my mission began. "I'm not sure," I said. "I still have a while to go on my mission. School, I guess."

"Probably the same," Chris said with no more passion than I had answered the question with.

"You don't sound very enthused about it," Rodney said. "How old are you guys, anyway?"

"I'm twenty," Chris said.

"I'll be twenty next month," I said.

"Twenty? Hell, when I was twenty I still hadn't joined the military yet. I'd been working at this assembly plant for two years, saving up money. One day I just walked in and quit. I didn't give two weeks' notice or nothin'. I just quit and I got in my car, got an oil change, got new tires, picked up my brother, Mark, and then hit the 35. You know, just drove all over the country for three months. Best time of my life. You two should do something like that."

"I've always wanted to do that," I said, looking at Chris. In fact, I was thinking how much I'd love to do it at that very moment—just pick up and go and not look back.

"Yeah. That'd be awesome," Chris told Rodney.

"You're twenty, for God's sake," Rodney said with more passion. "Get out there and live a little bit. Do drugs, get drunk, black out and not remember where you are the next morning. Have sex with girls, have sex with guys—hell, have sex with both at the same time. These are the things that you need to do. You need to break into a library and steal the entire collection of Hans Christian Andersen books. Get arrested, go to jail and spend the night there. You know, have some life experiences. Eat Taco Bell!"

We laughed. I thought about how romantic it all sounded, except for the getting-arrested part.

Rodney cocked his head and regarded us for a moment. "Something's different with you two," he said. "Seriously, ever since the first time I met you. I noticed things are different now. What's going on?"

"What do you mean?" I asked.

"Well, you two seem to be of a slightly different disposition now than you were then."

I looked at Chris, as if asking for permission to reveal our secret. But he didn't wait for an answer before reaching over and taking my hand in his own. Chris turned and looked into my eyes. We both looked back at Rodney without saying a word.

"Huh. I see how it is," Rodney said as he contemplated what we were telling him. He spoke without any apparent judgment.

"I hope it doesn't make you uncomfortable," Chris said.

"You kidding? Nothing gayer than the military. You should see some of the things I saw. Ain't nobody straight in a foxhole."

We all began to laugh.

"I can't believe this, you know," he continued. "I got these two queer, pot-smoking Mormons sitting here in my living room, eating tacos."

Chris and I laughed again. It *was* pretty funny. I began laughing so hard I had tears in my eyes.

"You okay, RJ?" Rodney asked after a moment.

"Yeah, yeah, yeah," I assured him.

"Look, boys," Rodney said. "I don't care if you're queer, straight, or if you prefer masturbation above all."

Chris giggled.

"You boys are all right with me."

We all laughed again. It felt so good to laugh. I hadn't wanted to acknowledge the anxiety I'd been feeling for the last couple of days, but it was just below the surface. The laughter helped defuse it. Whatever our visits offered Rodney, he was probably doing more for us than we were for him at that point.

"All right, well," Rodney said at last, picking up the Book of Mormon from the table. "You still want me to read this book?"

CHAPTER 21

I WOKE on my back, wearing only the bottoms to my temple garments. It was just after nine o'clock. I didn't move. Sunlight bathed me in a soothing warmth I was reluctant to interrupt. Chris lay naked beside me, his head resting on my chest. I stroked his hair, softly so as not to wake him. I'd never been so happy in my life. I wanted this moment to last forever. I loved waking up like this. With any luck I could go back to sleep and do it a second time. I closed my eyes and soon began to drift.

The next thing I knew, my eyes popped open. Had I heard something? The creak of floorboards, maybe? I sensed something. Chris was still asleep. I lifted my head, just in time to see Elder Harris enter from the hallway. Harris stopped abruptly and we made eye contact. Just then Chris woke as well and looked up, first at me, then tracing my gaze across the room to Harris.

Harris looked away, turned resolutely, and began to leave. I pushed my still-groggy companion aside and bolted for the door through which Harris had already exited. I flew into the hallway after him. "Wait!" I shouted to Harris.

Harris paused briefly but did not look back.

"Wait," I said again.

Harris continued walking. He turned the corner into the stairwell and was gone.

I considered following, but my lack of clothing made that impossible. Besides, what would I say? It was too late. This couldn't be explained, at least not in terms Harris—or the mission president— would understand.

I turned and walked back into the apartment, where I found Chris sitting on the edge of the bed, trembling.

"Why didn't you lock the door?" I barked. If only he had, this disaster could have been averted.

"I thought I did."

"Well, you obviously didn't, Chris, because our zone leader just walked in on us in bed together." I was in a panic. "What are we going to do?"

"I don't know."

I began to pace. "Goddammit!"

"Don't—"

"What, say the Lord's name in vain?"

"Yeah, because I'm still Mormon."

"And so am I," I said. "But my perspective has changed a little since we started this."

"Well, maybe mine hasn't changed as much as yours," Chris said bitterly.

"What do you mean?"

"Maybe you're a bigger faggot than I am." He spat the word.

I flew at him. In an instant I had him pinned to the bed on his back; I was astride him, our noses an inch apart. We'd been in this position before but never in anger. I burned with a rage that was foreign to me. The intensity of my own fury frightened me. I rolled off Chris and stood up. Neither of us spoke.

I retreated to the kitchen to get a grip on my emotions. I'd never been so infuriated in my life. At least not like this. Sure, I'd been pissed off plenty of times, and I'd said much worse than *goddammit* on occasion. But the depth of my passion at that moment was something I'd never experienced before. What Chris had said was more than just name-calling. It was personal. It went deep. Because, I realized, I loved Chris. I had trusted him with my deepest feelings. Hearing that word from him was a profound betrayal. I was both hurt and angry. Was that what it meant to be in love?

I had no doubt the other shoe would drop as soon as Elder Harris got ahold of the mission president. My remaining time there with Chris could probably be measured in minutes—certainly no more than a couple of hours. I couldn't let it end like that. If there was any chance to fix this, it would have to be now.

When I returned to the other room, Chris wasn't there. For a moment I panicked. Had he left? But no, he'd been completely naked; he couldn't have dressed and gone that fast. Besides, I would have heard the front door. He had to be in the bathroom.

I knocked lightly on the door. "Chris? You okay?" There was no answer. "Look, Chris. I'm really, truly sorry. I didn't mean to frighten you." There was still no answer. I tried the door; it was locked. I was relieved. At least that meant Chris hadn't left. Still, we needed to talk before the zone leaders came back to split us up.

I wanted to plead with Chris, but I decided it was best not to pressure him. He couldn't stay in there forever. I returned to the bed and began making it, partly out of nervous energy but also because I wanted to erase the evidence before Elder Harris returned with Elder Schmidt. I could imagine the image that was probably burned into the zone leader's head. No point in reminding him of it.

I was just smoothing the last of the wrinkles out of the bedspread when Chris emerged from the bathroom and crossed the room toward me.

"RJ, I'm sorry," he began, and then he burst into tears.

I went to him and threw my arms around him. "It's okay, Chris," I told him. "We'll be all right."

"But how?" Chris blubbered. The rest of what he was trying to say was lost in my shoulder, where his face was buried. We held each other tight, as though our lives depended on it. Tears began to flow from my eyes as well. For several minutes we just stood there, locked in what might be the last embrace we would ever share.

It wasn't long, however, before my tears evaporated into defiance. *No. This will* not *be our final embrace*, I told myself. *Not if I can help it.*

THE TENSION in the Mission Home was palpable as I waited for the inevitable. Beyond a curt nod or hello when I arrived, none of the staff elders had said a word to me that hadn't been absolutely necessary. They didn't even make eye contact with me, though I could feel them stealing looks at me when I wasn't looking directly at them.

I couldn't really blame them, though. What were they to think? They'd been taught the same thing I had: that homosexuality was sinful and unnatural. And even though the church had eased up in recent years, allowing that a person could be gay without "doing" gay and still be blameless for his condition, I was willing to bet none of my fellow missionaries knew anyone who was openly gay. Or if they did, they weren't friends with them.

Now they not only had a fellow missionary before them who was gay, but one who had *done* gay—with another missionary, no less. Even among those in the church who were inclined to be forgiving, sex of any kind outside of marriage was unquestionably a violation of one's temple covenants. So I wasn't expecting to find any compassion.

Far more uncomfortable for me than the reception in the office had been the absolutely silent drive to get there with Elder Harris. In fact, beyond the phone call instructing me to pack my things and await his and Schmidt's arrival, Harris hadn't said more than five words to me. On top of that, for the last fifteen minutes I'd been sitting not five feet from him as he pretended to read a Book of Mormon from the outer office's display table.

I wondered what was going through Marshall Harris's calculating little mind. For him, Chris's and my forbidden relationship wasn't an abstract concept; he had actually seen Chris's naked body pressed up against mine on the bed. Poor guy must be traumatized. Or maybe aroused. Who knew? The man was so hard to read.

Despite my situation, I wasn't at all sorry for the relationship I had with Chris. It felt far too right deep down inside to deny. But I *was* sorry for those who would never understand and for whom the knowledge would be difficult: my family, my friends, my priesthood leaders, and, yes, even my fellow missionaries.

The door to President Pierce's office opened, and one of his assistants walked out, signaling to me that I should enter. I felt all eyes on me as I walked inside and closed the door behind me. I'd known since my first kiss with Chris that this moment would come; still, the butterflies in my stomach were working overtime. I took a deep breath.

"Hello, Elder," President Pierce said.

"Hello."

"Please, have a seat," Pierce said. I sat. "Well, I'll get right to it. Elder Harris reported to me that yesterday he knocked on your door, then proceeded to enter your quarters."

Pierce paused before continuing. I could tell he was having a hard time stating what had happened without actually having to discuss it.

"Now I don't know how this happened, and I honestly don't care," he went on. "But I can only assume there is more to the story than unorthodox sleeping arrangements."

I nodded. I wasn't going to try to deny the truth.

"I was also recently made aware of your incessant absence in both church and missionary meetings." President Pierce looked at me accusingly. "Now, I find this behavior unacceptable and ungodly. You are not here to entertain any subconscious perversions you may be holding." He pronounced the word *perversions* as though it left a nasty taste in his mouth. "As a missionary, you have done these things in the eyes of our Heavenly Father while serving your church."

I did not refute that either. It was absolutely true.

"I have spoken to your stake president about this. I suggest you stop wasting your parents' money, go home, and deal with these issues. Be with your family and make things right with God."

Pierce sighed but did not continue. He had said his piece and seemed relieved not to have to mention any details of what so obviously disgusted him.

When I failed to say anything, he continued. "So, Richard, do you have anything you'd like to say?"

"No," I said, noting that, for the first time, President Pierce addressed me by my first name rather than as *Elder*. It was as though he had already symbolically stripped me of my priesthood office.

"Thank you. And God bless you," President Pierce said, not standing or offering his hand. It was a small omission, but a lifetime of church meetings had conditioned me to recognize that a priesthood leader who withheld his hand did not do so unintentionally. The mission president had just dissed me twice within a minute.

I got up and headed for the door.

"Oh, and could you send in Elder Harris on your way out?" Pierce called after me. "Thank you."

CHAPTER 22

I WALKED into the house and put my luggage down in the entry hall. I had refused an offer by my father to come pick me up at the airport, opting instead to take a shuttle. I knew my father would have a lot to say about my situation, and I hadn't wanted to discuss it while captive in the car with him. Besides, we needed to look each other in the eye for the conversation I'd been rehearsing all the way back to Idaho Falls.

I took a deep breath. The familiar scent of home caught me off guard. It was at once comforting and saddening. I was not the same son who had left that house just a few months earlier. That life was over. I couldn't bring it back. My relationship with my family would forever be altered by the events in Clackamas Falls.

I firmed up my resolve and walked into the kitchen where, despite the lateness of the hour, my father waited at the table.

"Hey, Dad."

"Hello, RJ. Your mom and sister are in bed."

"Okay."

"Hungry?" he asked, gesturing to a steaming bowl of mac 'n' cheese he'd just pulled out of the microwave.

"Yeah, thanks." I pulled out the chair opposite his and sat. No sooner had I taken my first bite than my father waded in.

"I spoke to the bishop a couple of days ago."

I stopped eating and looked him in the eye. I told myself yet again that I would not back down. My love for Chris was real, and it was good. I would not be talked out of that belief. I loved my father, but that could not change who I was.

"We had a long conversation," he went on. "He told me a story about a young man who came to him before his mission. Told him about thoughts he was having… toward other boys. 'Go on your mission,' the bishop told him. 'You'll come back, you'll meet a wife, you'll be fine.'"

My father paused and looked deep into my eyes, emphasizing his message.

"He also said he didn't need to mention it to anyone else. The Lord has a way of working these things out in due time. Well, that young missionary came back after serving an honorable mission. He went to the bishop and said he was still having these thoughts, but he listened to his mentors. As they said, once he met the right girl, everything would change. And he met a beautiful young woman three months later. They were married within six months, had their first child by the end of the year, second child the year after."

"Dad, I don't know what to say." I really didn't know. Was my father talking about himself? How was I supposed to respond to that? And even if he wasn't, his point was clear: he wanted me to pretend nothing had happened—pretend I wasn't gay, marry a woman.

"There's nothing to say, RJ. I went on a mission. I wanted you to go on one so you could have some of those experiences and we could sit at this table one day and talk about them."

"But, Dad, I did go on a mission, and I did have some of those experiences, and I truly did enjoy it."

"I know you did, son. It's just…. Dang it, Ricky! You're a winner, a champion. Now, you chose to do your missionary work, and that's very respectable but, son, you've got some hard choices to make. Choices that are going to affect your future. It's going to be hard on all of us."

I resisted the urge to object to my father's portrayal of the family as victims of my choices. But it was offensive to me nonetheless. My father was pretty much telling me they were ashamed of who I was.

"Ricky, this town and the church know everything about you. You think they're not going to find out what happened in Oregon?"

"I know they will." My tone was resolute. I would stand my ground.

"So what are you going to do?"

"Nothing."

"Nothing?"

"I'm going to let people's imaginations run rampant." That was a provocation, I knew, but I couldn't help myself. My father considered this to be a mess of my making, and one I needed to clean up. I would not stand for that characterization of who I was and who

I loved. My father needed to understand that, even if it meant I had to take a tough-love approach to get the message across to him.

Predictably, he was distressed by my reply. "Why would you do that?" he asked, although his expression was more perplexed than angry.

"I don't owe anybody an explanation," I shot back, defiant.

He looked away, struggling to stay in control before replying. "You're my son, and I love you first and foremost," he said with practiced determination. "But I cannot stand by you on this. Your family can't stand by you." When I didn't respond to the provocation, he continued. "So what are you going to do?"

I said nothing.

"Will you at least try to keep your focus and maintain your standing in the church? Will you?" He was pleading. I hated to see him like that. My dad was a good man, a man of character, but he still had a few things to learn, especially when it came to his son.

"I don't see how I can," I said. "I don't think the church helps the members have empathy for people like me." I hadn't rehearsed an explanation; it was a simple truth that had just descended upon me.

"People like *you*?" he protested. "Ricky, there's only ever been speculation."

I interrupted. "Speculation? Dad, I'm gay. I didn't choose this, Dad. It's been in me for a long time." The starkness of the admission caught me off guard, and I began to choke up. This was the core truth we'd been dancing around. And neither of us had spoken it until now. This was not a phase, no minor anomaly in the life of his otherwise perfect little boy. I was a gay man, and we both needed to confront that fact before we could move forward.

My father remained silent for a long moment. I waited.

"Okay," he said at last, getting up from the table, defeated.

I watched with tears in my eyes as he walked out of the room without looking back. I pushed the unfinished bowl of food away and propped my elbows on the table. I buried my face in my hands as quiet sobs overcame me.

CHAPTER 23

THE NEXT day was no easier. I had an afternoon appointment with the stake president, the outcome of which was entirely predictable. What was less certain was how my mother, my sister, and Elise would react to the news. My mother already knew why I'd been sent home early; Mary Anne and Elise did not.

Saturday morning breakfast had always been a family affair. This was no different, although the conversation was clearly contorting itself to avoid the very large elephant in the room. My dad worked on the waffles as though they were a priceless foreign sports car, my mom offered more servings of orange juice than any family could possibly need, and we all sat at the table politely discussing Mary Anne's coursework for the upcoming semester at BYU-Idaho with a peculiar fascination. I could hardly wait for the ordeal to end.

After I had finished washing the dishes, a task I volunteered for because I needed a few minutes alone to clear my head, I went to find my mom. As usual on a Saturday, she was out tending the garden. Today she seemed to be working particularly hard at it, swinging a pickax at a stubborn stump she was trying to remove. I couldn't help but wonder if she too was working off the nervous tension that had taken hold of the whole family in the hours since my return.

"Hey, Mom," I said as I approached. "You want me to help you with that?"

"No thanks, Ricky," she said, resting the pick at her side. "I'll get it eventually." She smiled. "It's just something I need to do."

I recognized the smile. It was the long-suffering smile I had always seen her put on when she'd just conceded an argument to Dad, part resignation and part quiet stoicism. She obviously needed to talk.

"Look, Mom," I said. "I know Dad has told you everything—"

She interrupted. "Honey, you don't have to explain. I'll still love you, no matter what."

"I know, Mom." I was already getting choked up again. "But you need to hear it from me, okay?"

"If that's what you want." She laid the tool against the fence and started toward a shaded bench in the corner of the garden. "You can talk to me whenever you want."

I followed and took a seat next to her on the bench. I watched as she took off her gardening gloves and absentmindedly smoothed her hair back, though it was already in a ponytail. I could tell she was nervous. I was too.

"Look, Mom," I began, "I know this isn't easy for you."

She turned to look at me with tears welling. "Oh, sweetie, you don't need to worry about me. But your father—"

"I know, Mom," I interrupted. "He's made it clear to me how he feels."

"Ricky, you have to be patient with him." My mother took my hand in hers. "It takes time to understand these things. They're new to us."

"Well, it's kinda new to me too," I said. "I mean, it's not like I've been planning this or anything."

"That's just what I'm saying, honey. None of us has planned for this. You've come to where you are over a long period of time. I have no doubt you've given it a lot of thought. You need to be willing to allow your father to give it the same amount of thought. It's as much an adjustment for him as it is for you."

"But what if he doesn't reach the same conclusion?" I said. "I can't live my life based on what he thinks."

"I'm not saying you should, Ricky," my mother said, squeezing my hand. "You just need to love him and help him adjust to this. Don't judge him any more harshly than you would have him judge you."

"I don't want to judge him, Mom," I said, pained at her indictment. I knew she had a point; I had been too critical of my father. "I just want us to be like before. I'm still the same person I've always been."

"Oh, Ricky," she said, hugging me close and putting my head to her shoulder. "Of course you are. And your father still loves you. Surely you know that?" She lowered her eyes to meet mine.

"Yeah, I know."

"And I love you too," she said, releasing all but my hand, which she held in both of her own. She looked at me for a second longer, as though she had more to say. But then she turned away, stifling tears.

"HEY, SIS," I said, tapping on Mary Anne's bedroom door and poking my head inside. "Got a minute?"

"Yeah, sure," she said, removing the iPod buds from her ears. She sat up and made room for me to join her on the bed. The look on her face told me she knew what this was about—maybe not the gay thing but the reason for my early return, at least. "What's up?" she asked as I sat down next to her.

I told Mary Anne everything. Well, almost everything. I spared her the details of my sexual involvement with Chris, but I made it clear to her I loved Chris very much, even now, and I was not sorry for that.

She responded without drama; she seemed neither upset nor judgmental. "It doesn't have to be anything serious, Ricky."

"What do you mean?"

"I mean, it could just be something that happens, you know, when missionaries have to spend every minute together. It doesn't make you gay."

I shook my head slowly. "No, sis. It's much more than that. Trust me."

"But it's not, like, permanent, right? Now that you're back here with Elise...." But she trailed off, correctly reading the look I was giving her. I was not being unkind to her, nor she to me. I understood her confusion. I'd shared it as far back as I could remember. It was only a moment before a full understanding washed over her. "Oh, Ricky." Mary Anne reached over and hugged me. "You know I love you, no matter what." Suddenly she pulled back with a look of concern.

"Oh my gosh, Ricky. What are you going to say to Elise?"

THAT, OF course, was the same question I had been wrestling with. And I still didn't have a good answer. For three years I let Elise believe a romantic future was possible for us. At times, I'd even believed it myself. I liked Elise a lot. I really did care for her in a way that went beyond simple friendship. But I now knew, all too well, that was not the same thing as physical attraction.

Until now it had been easy to simulate romance—heck, that was the only kind of romance the church allowed, so I'd never been under any pressure to prove anything. We'd kissed and held hands, taken long walks together, snuggled in front of the TV for a PG-rated movie or two.

Even the dry-humping we'd tried once or twice was a way of testing myself. I had become suspicious of my own lack of physical response to Elise. Then, after the incident in Hope Grove, I had been desperate to force a response, to prove to myself that I wasn't "that way." But there had been no response.

Poor Elise had no way of knowing my intentions toward her were any different than any other "normal" boy's. She had every reason to believe the physical closeness we shared was evidence of my attraction, and that someday we might make it official. She had intimated as much when she told me she would wait for me while I served my mission.

Coming out to my family was one thing; they would always be there, even through the rough patches. But telling Elise was different; it would likely end our friendship. She would have a legitimate cause to feel betrayed, and I wouldn't blame her if she hated me. I had led her on for three years with false expectations. I deserved to feel guilty, and I did.

We were finishing the chicken salad sandwiches I'd fixed for lunch. While we ate we'd talked about everything but why I had come home early from my mission. She must have been dying to know, but she hadn't asked. That's the way she was. So patient and passive. For a moment I was tempted to resent her for that. Why didn't she just come out and challenge me? Wouldn't it be easier if she just yelled at me and demanded to know?

But there she sat on the couch, looking sweet, giving me the loving smile she always gave me. And I was going to have to be the one to break her heart. Darn her!

"Listen, Elise," I said, my head bowed. "I've got to tell you something. And it's not easy." I looked up at her. She looked at me lovingly, still smiling, but her brow furrowed. It was obvious to her, as it was to everyone, that my early return did not bode well, and that bad news was inevitable.

I took a deep breath and jumped in with both feet. "The reason they sent me home is because I'm gay."

In the instant before she looked away, I saw a flicker of the tears to come.

"I'm sorry, Elise," I said, wanting to comfort her but not knowing how. "I know this is sudden, but I didn't know how else to—"

She was already shaking her head. "No, RJ. Don't say any more."

"I really—"

But she threw up a hand. "No." She still wouldn't look at me.

I sat helplessly, silenced and awkward.

"I had heard the rumors," she said. "But I didn't want to believe them." She spun to look at me. "I had to hear you say it."

I took her hand. "I'm sorry, I should have—"

She jerked her hand away. "No," she said, shaking her head more vigorously now. "No, don't."

I wanted to soften the blow for her somehow. "I still care about you, though. That counts for something, doesn't it?"

I tried to take her hand again, but she pushed me away. She was crying and again refused to look at me. I didn't know what else to say. We sat that way, silent, for several awkward minutes. "Elise," I said finally, trying to get her to look at me.

Abruptly she got up from the couch and made for the front door. I followed, calling her name, but she didn't stop. I stood in the doorway and watched, helpless, as she got into her car and drove away. I felt like shit.

CHAPTER 24

THE PURPOSE of the meeting with President Whitmer that morning did not need to be spelled out to me. Every Mormon knew what the process was when you broke the big rules; it was engrained. When a priesthood holder had committed a "serious sin"—which usually meant either something sexual in nature or involving prison time—a meeting of the stake high council would be convened to deliberate that person's membership in the church. Excommunication was almost always the result.

The last chance to avoid that outcome was in a private interview with the stake president, such as the one I was having today. If I showed enough contrition for my sin and expressed a commitment to repentance, high council proceedings might be avoided.

But I knew I couldn't do that. There would be no leniency for me. How could I repent of who I was? How could I beg forgiveness for loving Chris? It would invalidate all we had shared; it would make a mockery of the depth of feeling we had for one another. Whatever happened in the stake president's office, I would not betray Chris; I would not betray myself.

"RJ, I'd like to start off with a prayer if that's okay," President Whitmer said once I was seated before him.

"Yes, sir." I bowed my head. I liked President Whitmer. I didn't want to show any disrespect, even if I had come here to stand up to him. I knew the man was only doing his job. We would both do what we had to do today, and then it would be over.

"Dear Heavenly Father, thank you for getting RJ here safely. We ask that you please bless this young man and guide him through this rough time, in the name of Jesus Christ. Amen."

"Amen." I looked up at him and did my best to maintain a neutral expression.

"RJ, I've known you since you were a child. I was at your baptism, I've watched you grow up, go to high school, college, and

I deemed you worthy to serve a mission." His tone was entirely congenial, without recrimination. He seemed pained to be having this conversation. He held up a sheet of paper and continued, "If anyone told me ten years ago that I would be looking at the words written here, I'd…." He took a new tack. "RJ, tell me, why are you here today, son?"

"To talk about my future as a member of the Church of Jesus Christ of Latter-day Saints," I said evenly.

"This is a very serious matter, you know this."

"Yes."

"And this could be grounds for excommunication. You're aware of that?"

"Yes."

"First off, I'd like for you to tell me in detail about the relationship between you and…." He paused, looking at the paper. "Elder Merrill."

I hesitated. The mission president hadn't asked for details—for which I had been grateful; I'd hoped President Whitmer wouldn't ask either. "I'm sorry," I told him. "I don't know if I can talk about this. It's… it's personal."

"You broke a very sacred law."

"You're right. I did. I can't deny that," I said. I tried to maintain an air of detachment, but I realized that was not going to be easy. Already my jaw was clenched and my breathing irregular.

He seemed perplexed. "Did you want to go on a mission?"

"Of course. I always have."

"And you wanted to serve, even though you knew this about yourself?"

"Yes," I said without hesitation. Whitmer didn't get it. Nobody in the church did. Gay boys in the church wanted nothing more than to be fully accepted, to be the best Mormons we could be, as if in doing so we could compensate for our aberrant sexuality, which we were powerless to change. "I'm not the first gay man you've sent on a mission," I told him. "And I won't be the last. The church doesn't do much to provide a way for us to be honest about it."

I looked away for a moment, summoning the courage to continue. "As for Elder Merrill, I will say this: Elder Merrill and I were mission companions. We served our church well. I cannot speak for him nor will I go into greater detail other than to say that I have great feelings for Elder Merrill." I felt my lip quiver, but I couldn't control it. "My feelings for him are greater than for any man." Tears welled up in my eyes.

"And if I acted upon my emotions, I don't see any injustice in my acts nor disgrace in them. Shame on you and shame on this church," I said, my voice breaking. The tears began to flow. "I was raised to believe I was part of something, beyond my family and friends, and now because of who I am, I don't get to be that. I'm excluded from that. I'm not sorry. I hope you know that. I am not sorry."

I hadn't meant to sound so defiant, but there it was. I'd been honest, and if that honesty was brutal, so be it. I looked him in the eye, even as my tears continued.

Whitmer was clearly moved by my emotion. There were tears in his eyes too. Still, my position left me no wiggle room.

Whitmer's response was no surprise to me. "Son, I want you to know that I am truly sorry for your pain. I'm sure you've heard it said that the church is a hospital for sinners, not a museum for saints. We are imperfect, both as a people and a church." Whitmer dabbed his eyes with a handkerchief. "But we must maintain order in the Lord's kingdom; and that requires that we live by rules. And in this case the rules are clear: I must convene the high council to consider your worthiness to remain a member of this church. Do you understand?"

I nodded and wiped a sleeve across my face. Whitmer pushed a box of tissues across the desk toward me.

"If you showed some remorse, however," he continued, "I would have some leeway...."

I shook my head. "I'm sorry, President Whitmer. I cannot be sorry for the love I have for Chris Merrill. You do whatever you have to do, but I can tell you this: I don't need a church court to validate what my heart tells me. I'm sorry to be so blunt, but that's God's honest truth."

MY FAMILY was waiting for me in the foyer of the stake center when I emerged from President Whitmer's office. My dad practically ran to me.

"How'd it go?" He was smiling, hope written large across his face.

"It went okay."

"So?" he persisted.

I wished I could let him down easy, but there was no way. "I told him I don't need to regain my worthiness, and that I don't need to see the high council either."

"What?" My father was crestfallen. He turned away in what I could only assume was an attempt to keep a lid on his anger, not given to outbursts of emotion. But I always knew when it simmered below the surface.

"Why not?" my mother asked. Despite her earlier expression of support, it was clear she had not expected this from me. Still, she hugged me and held me close.

I was genuinely touched—and began to get choked up again. Then Mary Anne rushed over and joined us in a three-way hug. I looked over both their shoulders to the far end of the foyer, where my father was pacing in obvious distress.

He turned and looked up and, seeing the familial display of love, hesitated only a moment before coming over to rejoin us. He put his hand on my shoulder. It was a conciliatory, if reluctant, gesture. But it was a start, I thought. It was all I could expect from my dad just then. Someday, I hoped, I would feel my father's full love and support again.

CHAPTER 25

THE FIRST thing I did when we got home from the stake center was lock myself in my room and pour out my heart in a letter to Chris. I could have tried to find an e-mail address, maybe through one of the elders back in Oregon, but I didn't want to involve anyone else. Besides, there was something romantic about getting a letter in the mail—a love letter, the kind you could tuck away in a shoebox and reread years later. Who ever went back and reminisced over an e-mail?

I wasn't even sure where Chris was at that moment. I assumed he was back in Salt Lake by then, but we had never thought to exchange home addresses. I imagined he was enduring inquisitions by church and family, similar to the ones I had endured. I wondered what answers he would give, especially with his dad being a General Authority. Would Chris defend our love as honestly and openly as I had?

I hated to think what the alternative might be. Maybe, under duress, he had recanted his love for me. Had he pledged to repent of who he was, who *we* were? There would certainly be a lot more pressure on him to do that than there was on me. The shame and embarrassment factor would be ten times greater. Living in Salt Lake would only make it worse.

I wished I could kidnap Chris and get him away from Salt Lake, take him someplace where there would be no pressure to go straight and get married, a place where people either understood or didn't care. I thought back to the fantasy Rodney had planted in our minds: a road trip. How cool would that be? Chris and I had talked about doing such a thing, but we'd never made any actual plans. Would Chris be willing?

*Wouldn't it be awesome if we could actually
take that road trip Rodney suggested? I would so love
to just be free of this whole judgment thing, just the*

two of us out there, discovering the world together.
Discovering ourselves.

I could easily get a good used car. My dad's a
mechanic, did I ever tell you that? We could do this
thing cheap, you know, take a tent and a couple of
sleeping bags. (Preferably the kind that zip together,
ha-ha!)

I don't know where you are or what's going on
with you right now, but I really want to see you again.
I'm sending this care of the mission home; I'm sure
they'll forward it to you. Let me know as soon as you
receive it, okay?

I love you, Chris. I need to hear from you. Tell
me you're okay.

All my love,
RJ

I sealed up the letter and addressed it to the Portland Mission Home. I hoped I could trust snail mail to remain confidential. Now that Chris and I were disgraced, somebody in the mission office might feel it his moral duty to monitor our correspondence. But with luck, the secretary would just go ahead and forward the letter to Chris's home address and we could begin corresponding directly.

I searched my mom's desk for a stamp and affixed it to the envelope. Even as I walked the letter out to the mailbox I was already impatient, wanting a response. This old-school method of communication would be torture. Maybe I should just e-mail, forget who might be monitoring it.

Eventually I resigned myself to the fact that I had to get my mind off Chris for a while and let the process unfold. It was time to do some serious thinking about my future, with or without Chris. So I did what I always did when reflection was called for: I went for a run. While I usually ran the Idaho Falls Greenbelt Trail, today I chose a different route. I didn't feel like seeing either the temple or Freeman Park. I wanted to clear my mind of the things they represented and try to get a fresh perspective on where I wanted my life to be headed.

I hadn't declared a major during my freshman year. I wasn't really sure what I wanted to do. Or what I was qualified to do. I was good at running and wrestling, but I couldn't really make a career out of either of those. I had thought about doing some kind of writing, maybe. I liked the idea of working in semisolitude. It wasn't that I was antisocial; it was just that it was easier to concentrate on something when I was alone. I wanted a career that allowed me some peace and quiet.

Like now, as I jogged through Tautphaus Park. As usual, it was nearly empty on a Sunday, thanks to the Mormon prohibition against violating the Sabbath with recreational activities. I'd known some guys in school who wouldn't go running on Sunday, but I'd always argued that if my body was God's temple, then it couldn't be a sin to take care of it. Back then, it'd been a cheeky joke, but now I reflected on the fact that my body was the only temple available to me. Excommunication would bar me from entering the one up the road, as well as all the others the church had built around the world.

I thought about life without the church; what would that look like? I thought back to an old missionary film the church used to show at the temple visitors' center. It was called *Man's Search for Happiness*. In it, people who rejected the Restored Gospel were depicted cavorting on a carnival midway, as though drunk and debauched, pure hedonists. But that wasn't me. I didn't find that at all attractive. The whole "sex, drugs, and rock and roll" meme just wasn't who I was.

Sex with Chris, of course, had been altogether different. It had been spiritual. It had brought us closer together. It was tender and caring. It was far from hedonistic. That was the only sex I wanted. Promiscuity didn't appeal to me. I didn't fit the gay stereotype the church and media presented. Neither did Chris. There had to be some other alternative.

With gay marriage gaining acceptance in so many places, I wondered if it would be possible for me to live that way someday. Could I marry a man and be happy? Could I marry Chris? It seemed preposterous. My family could never accept that; I'd be cut off from them, in this life as well as in the eternities. And Chris? There was no way his family would tolerate such blatant defiance of church teachings. He'd be disowned for sure. I couldn't ask that of him, even if I was willing to endure it.

I wanted my family, my church, *and* Chris, all at the same time. If only that were possible. It was obvious the church had already slipped from my grasp, though that didn't mean I had to abandon the principles with which I'd been raised. My family would struggle, but I was sure they'd be there for me in the end. That left Chris. What did Chris want? The answer to that would have to wait.

THE RETURN letter from Chris came far sooner than I dared to hope; barely a week had passed since I'd mailed mine. I burst through the front door, threw the rest of the day's mail on the kitchen counter, and raced down the hall to my bedroom. I was trembling with anticipation as I closed the door and threw myself across my bed with the cherished letter in hand. I slipped a thumb under the sealed flap and carefully tore the envelope open. I took a deep breath and removed a single handwritten page.

> *Dear RJ,*
> *Thank you so much for your letter. You don't*
> *know how much it means to me to hear from you.*

Yes, I do, I thought. *I so do.*

> *You asked where I am. I'm still here in Oregon,*
> *where you left me, though I've been transferred*
> *to the mission office to serve as a clerk. The only*
> *explanation I can find for my not being sent home like*
> *you is that my father must have interceded to keep me*
> *here. Not out of any particular approval of me, but*
> *rather to protect his own reputation, I am certain.*

Oh my gosh, I thought. What must that be like? With everyone knowing what happened? How could he face the other missionaries? How could he look Harris in the eye? Or President Anderson?

*I suppose it really is for the best, though. I only
have ten weeks left to complete my mission, and if I
do, then there will be far fewer questions to answer
down the road from nosy church members who would
wonder why a General Authority's son came home
early.*

*My father wants to drive out here to pick me
up when I'm released in August. But there's no way I
could handle twenty hours of talking about this, with
no way to escape his scrutiny. I'm going to need some
time before I'm ready to face him.*

*I too think about that little road trip that
Rodney suggested. The one where we'd break into
a library and steal the Hans Christian Andersen
collection. Ha!*

*I miss you so much, RJ. I can't wait to see you
again. I hope it's soon.*

Love,
Chris

I could barely read the last few lines through the blur of my
tears. I wiped a sleeve across my eyes and read the entire letter again.
And then a third time. It was as though I was afraid someone might
hit the Delete key and those happy words would vanish, taking my joy
along with them. But they were real, and they were in Chris's voice,
echoing through my head.

I rolled over on my back and stared at the ceiling. Its emptiness
became a blank canvas on which I could plan my future with Chris.
I would go to Portland and pick him up, I decided. I would rescue
him from the drive home with his father, and we'd make that road
trip a reality.

I had ten weeks to find the perfect used car. My father could
help me, but I would refrain from telling him what I intended to do
with it.

CHAPTER 26

CHRIS'S LETTERS, which came without fail each Wednesday, kept my spirits up. As his release date neared, my excitement grew. I hadn't mentioned the road trip again—nor had he—but I did tell him I'd like to come see him in Portland when he was released. We could talk about the road trip once I got there. There was no hurry.

In the meantime, we wrote to each other about our day-to-day experiences. Chris's position in the mission office gave him access to all the latest gossip, which I found amusing. At times it was affirming, as well. I took comfort in the fact that Chris and I were far from the only rule-breakers in the Oregon Portland Mission. It seemed the straight elders had plenty of difficulty with chastity as well, so it wasn't something they could pin on us for being gay.

Two weeks before I was due to leave for Portland, I still didn't have a car, and I began to worry that I'd have to spend a lot more money than I'd intended. So when one of my father's clients couldn't pay his repair bill and forfeited his beat-up 1992 Chevy Blazer as payment, I jumped at it. For only the cost of parts—my dad didn't charge me for the labor—paid for with money remaining in my mission fund, I had a decent set of wheels.

I immediately set out to fill my new car with supplies for my adventure with Chris. First, however, I needed to break the news to my father that I was leaving. I had intended to say something sooner, but it never seemed like the right time before. Of course, I told him only that I intended to take a road trip; I said nothing about taking Chris along.

"Ricky," he said, shaking his head the way he always did when he was disappointed with his children. "You're an adult now—you can do as you like. But I've got to say that this is a terribly irresponsible use of your mission fund. I would have expected you to apply that money to your education."

"But, Dad, the trip will be an education. Besides, I've still got the merit scholarship," I countered. "That'll cover books and tuition. I'll get a job spring semester to cover living expenses."

"But, son, you need to focus on your coursework—"

"It's okay, Dad. I'll make it all work out. Besides, that money was intended to pay for me to go out and share my testimony, right?"

"I don't see how this relates to that."

"Well, for starters, I'm heading back to Clackamas Falls to see people I taught, like Rodney, the guy we tracted out during my first month in the field. You know, I wrote to you about him. That's still missionary work, right?"

"In a sense, I suppose," he conceded. He seemed to soften a bit.

"And then I'll be meeting new people wherever I go," I continued. "In a way, that's what this trip is about—seeing new places, meeting new people. Everyone I talk to will be learning something about Mormons. I'll kind of be a missionary-at-large."

"I wouldn't go that far, Ricky," he said with a smirk. "But I get your point. I just don't want to see you wasting that money. Remember, your sister sacrificed to raise some of it."

"I've already talked to Mary Anne and offered to pay back her share of it. She said she won't need a car in Rexburg. She thinks this is a great idea. Besides, I'm going to be really frugal. I'm planning to camp most of the time and rely on the kindness of strangers. You know, like the apostles did."

"Son, you'd better stop before you really scare me." My father laughed. "I don't want to imagine you out there on street corners begging for food and shelter."

My mother was characteristically supportive, if not overjoyed at the idea of her son vagabonding about the country. I assured her I wasn't going to be panhandling or sleeping on the street. "I can definitely afford campgrounds," I told her.

"Do what makes you happy, honey. I just want you to be safe" was her final pronouncement on the subject.

All of this, of course, was a carefully constructed narrative designed to reassure my parents. It wasn't a lie; I'd be doing everything I said I would. I just failed to mention Chris, and the fact that getting to know my boyfriend better was the primary focus of the journey. Still,

I would be meeting people along the way. And whatever impression they got of Mormonism would not be a misrepresentation. Chris was still a Mormon, and I considered myself one too, even if the church had turned its back on me.

Chris's release was set for a Monday afternoon. I didn't want to waste money on an overnight stay the night before, so I chose to begin my ten-hour drive at 3:00 a.m. that same morning. One advantage of this schedule was that there would be no dramatic farewell scene with my family. I simply said my good-byes after Sunday dinner and was in bed by seven.

Eight hours later I was cranking the stereo as I pulled onto I-15 southbound for my seven-hundred-mile journey, the first leg of which would be an unprecedented adventure. The freeway lighting in town gradually ceded its illumination to the darkness of less-populated territory. An hour later, as I reached Pocatello and veered west on I-86, the waxing moon had moved high enough above the horizon to trace silhouettes on the expanding landscape, and the canopy of stars was revealed in its fullness. I was exhilarated to finally be making my escape!

I'd checked and double-checked my list of camping supplies a half-dozen times before I left. Still, my mind drifted back to the inventory I had packed into the Blazer: tent, two sleeping bags and ground cloths, ice chest, electric and gas lanterns, four flashlights, propane cook stove, a case of Sterno, aluminum plates, cups, and utensils. There were towels and soap and sanitizer, a collapsible shovel, plastic garbage bags, a first aid kit, and three cases of water.

Chris, of course, would have to buy some new clothes before we hit the road. I had his wardrobe memorized; outside of white shirts and ties, he had only one pair of jeans, two pairs of running shorts, and two T-shirts. I smiled as I pictured Chris stretching in his shorts and favorite T. All those mornings we had gone running together, sometimes falling into sweaty, passionate lovemaking as soon as we returned to the apartment. It seemed so long ago. Never had I missed anybody as much as I missed Chris. I got aroused at the mere thought that we'd be reunited in a matter of hours.

For the next eight hours my thoughts drifted back and forth between the past and the future. Beneath the surface I knew the road trip, however long it lasted, would not be forever. I first had to convince Chris to take the leap with me. But I was sure if he wasn't ready to see his father, this would be a good way for him to prepare. We needed to learn to be ourselves, to like ourselves, before we could successfully stand up to those who would try to convince us we were godless sinners.

The day would come, of course, when we would again have to confront the harsh realities of family, work, school, and church, all of which could be hostile to our relationship. But there would be time enough to worry about those challenges later. At the moment, the world was ours; the sky was the limit.

CHAPTER 27

PORTLAND INTERNATIONAL was a zoo. I hadn't considered the Monday habits of business travelers when I told Chris I'd meet him there. I was about ready to start swinging at the swarms of people who got between me and the food court, where Chris was waiting for me, so crazy was I with anticipation.

And then I saw him. Almost before I could register the thought, my vision blurred with moisture. Breaking out of the crowd, I sprinted the last fifty feet. Chris saw me coming and he jumped. He opened his arms wide to greet me. Our embrace was immediate and impregnable, as though a quantum bond had just produced a new element.

"It's so good to see you," I said as I buried my face in Chris's neck.

"You too," Chris said, squeezing me hard enough to knock the wind out of me.

Tears poured from both of us. Neither let go for nearly a minute. I was in no hurry to disengage; we had all the time in the world. At last we pulled back just enough to look each other in the eye. I could not restrain myself; in a split second we were lip-locked. Chris reacted stiffly at first but yielded quickly. Another hug followed, and then another shorter kiss.

"Wow," Chris said as we finally disengaged. "That's quite a hello." He laughed and shuffled his feet, glancing from side to side, embarrassed. "I'm not quite sure these folks were quite ready for that."

"As if!" I replied with a laugh. "This is Portland!"

Chris nodded toward the passing throngs. "Yeah, but at least half these people aren't from here."

"Well, they'll get used to it," I said. "I'm so over worrying about what people think."

"Uh, hello?" Chris said. "Look how I'm dressed. I don't think anyone's going to get used to man-on-missionary snogging anytime soon."

"Not to worry," I said with a smile. "I'll have you out of those clothes before long." I grabbed one of Chris's two suitcases. "C'mon. Let's go shopping."

"Wait, what?" Chris said. He pretended to be astonished, but I was pretty sure he had an idea of what I had planned.

"We're taking a little vacation," I said without missing a beat. "Just you and me."

"RJ, that's crazy. I've got a plane ticket." He gestured toward the gate. "My flight leaves in two hours."

"So you can get a full refund—well, minus a small fee. And when you're ready to go back to Salt Lake, I can drop you off there." I knew he'd go for that, but not without first putting up the "responsible behavior" front I knew him so well for.

He didn't disappoint in that regard. "RJ, that would be a totally irresponsible thing to do. You know that."

"Yeah," I conceded. "Plus, it'll be totally fun. C'mon, let's get going." I turned and began walking.

"RJ!" Chris snapped. He was exasperated, not angry. "Just wait a minute, would you?"

I stopped. "What?"

"Let's at least spend some time talking before we go rushing off like fools. C'mon, you can buy me lunch," he said with a wink. He strode past me toward the food court vendors. I happily followed. I had him and I knew it.

After lunch, I let Chris use my phone to e-mail his dad and tell him he wouldn't be on the plane, and then we headed out to the mall to get Chris some civilian clothes. Once he'd shed the missionary getup, we did the grocery shopping for our road trip.

Before we left, however, we would pay a visit to Rodney.

"So he knows we're coming by?" Chris asked. "You've kept in touch?"

"Yep. He's been looking forward to it," I told him. "Says he's got some news for us."

"Well, if he expects us to get high again, I'm going to have to pass," Chris said, unloading the grocery cart. "That stuff makes me paranoid, and I'm already a nervous wreck about doing this."

"Yeah, I think I'll pass too," I agreed. "I don't plan to start this trip with a DUI." I gave his arm a squeeze. "And this is going to be the best decision you ever made, trust me."

Thirty minutes later we rolled to a stop in front of Rodney's new place in Clackamas Falls.

"This already looks a lot nicer than the old place," I said as we got out of the car. "It couldn't possibly smell as bad, at least."

Chris laughed. "You got that right!"

I rang the bell and we waited. I turned to Chris. "Déjà vu, right?"

Chris smiled. "Yeah. Just like the first time. That seems years ago already."

The door opened. It was as though we'd never been away. There stood Rodney, as always, in his bathrobe, unshaven, hair tousled, giving us that trademark sardonic half smile.

"Hey there, boys," he said. "It's good to see you all again." He turned from the door and headed back to his recliner.

It might have been a new apartment, I noted, but it was the same recliner. I looked around. Much of the décor was the same as well. At least it didn't smell. Chris and I took up our usual positions on the couch.

"So you guys like the new place?" Rodney asked.

"It's great," Chris said.

"Yeah, it's really nice," I agreed.

"Thank you. Yeah, there's only so much mold and roaches a man can handle. Had to get out of that other place."

Chris and I both nodded our agreement.

"So," Rodney continued. "RJ tells me you guys are making a run for it, huh?"

"Yeah," Chris and I said in unison.

"Well, I hope this wasn't too much of a detour."

"Not a problem at all," I said.

"Yeah, it's fine," Chris agreed.

"We're starting out at the coast—that's only a couple of hours away," I added. "Besides, you were a huge inspiration for this."

"Yeah, definitely," Chris assured him.

"Well, good," Rodney said. "All I did was get you high and make you watch movies with me. But, okay, I'll take the credit."

We all laughed.

"Those were some good times," he said.

"Yeah," Chris said. "I think it was a major turning point for both of us." He turned to me and squeezed my hand.

"Hey," Rodney said, acknowledging our display of affection with a nod. "I wanna let you guys know that if ever you wanna make out in front of me, it's okay."

"What?" Chris said, looking from Rodney to me and back again.

"I'm just saying that if… if ever you get the urge to climb on top of RJ and start making out with him, it's okay. I want you two to be comfortable here in my new home. It's your home too."

"That's good to know, Rodney. Thank you," I said. The guy was as loopy as I remembered him. At other times, though, he could be unexpectedly poignant. I figured it was probably due to the drugs.

"That's kind of creepy, actually," Chris said. He laughed uncomfortably.

"Is it?" Rodney said. "I'm sorry." After an awkward pause, he continued. "Well, I've got some big news. You ready?"

"Yeah," Chris said.

Rodney held out a pipe he'd picked up from the table. "Here, hit this first."

"I don't know," Chris said, hesitating. He looked at me for support.

"C'mon," Rodney prodded. "Trust me. You need some for this." Then, as if suddenly coming awake, he added, "You still look like a missionary, Chris."

Chris laughed. "Yeah. We just bought some new clothes. I need to change."

"Well, you can do it here if you like," Rodney said, still holding the pipe toward me. "But let's take care of first things first."

Chris relented and hit the pipe. He offered it to me. I was about to decline, but Rodney jumped in. "You too, RJ. It's the price of admission to my little carnival here."

I accepted the pipe and took a pull. After setting it back on the table, I turned to Rodney. "Okay. So what is it?"

Rodney did a drum roll on the table edge. "I'm going to die," he deadpanned.

"Are you serious?" I asked. The news took me by surprise. Chris looked equally dumbstruck.

Rodney nodded. "Yes, sir. It might not be tomorrow, it might not be next week, but one day sooner rather than later I'm going to die." He motioned to the pipe. "You done with that?"

I picked up the pipe and handed it to him. I still wasn't sure what to make of what he was telling us. "I can't tell if you're joking," I said.

"I'm not joking," Rodney said without inflection.

"What is it?" I asked.

Rodney took a long drag on the pipe before responding. "Cancer."

We were stunned. Chris looked at me, then back at Rodney. "What kind of cancer?" he asked.

"The kind that kills you."

CHAPTER 28

THE GRAVITY of Rodney's news kept us at his place longer than we had intended. We ordered in pizza and stayed up talking and toking well beyond dark.

Rodney talked of his childhood, of his close relationship with his mother, Gloria, about his estrangement and eventual abandonment by his father. But what consumed Rodney most, and seemed to lie at the heart of his PTSD, was the loss of his brother, Mark. Rodney could not let it go. It haunted his dreams and stalked his waking hours. Both Chris and I developed an even deeper love and empathy for Rodney that evening. It made a permanent impression on both of us. Coupled with the news of Rodney's terminal diagnosis, the visit left us in a very dark place that night.

By the time we left, neither of us was in any shape for a drive to the coast, let alone setting up a campsite, so we splurged on a room at the Drake Hotel in the center of town. I had been imagining for months the passion-filled hours we would share on our first night back together. But the reality was that neither of us was in the mood for sex, a result of our grief for Rodney coupled with too much pot. Instead we brushed our teeth, stripped to our temple garments, and wrapped ourselves together in the bedcovers, just as we had done while missionary companions.

Chris rested his head on my chest. "You're still wearing your garments," he noted with bemusement.

"Yeah," I said. "I figure my relationship with God is up to me, not the church. They may have turned their back on me, but that doesn't mean I have to kick God out of my life."

"I can respect that," he said without judgment. "But what meaning do the garments have for you? I mean, now that you could be stripped of your priesthood, your washing and anointing, your endowment, everything?"

"Think about it, Chris," I said. I wasn't bothered by the question. In fact, I enjoyed having this discussion with someone who could understand what I was going through, someone I loved. "Do you remember what the garment symbols stand for?"

"Yeah, sure."

"The compass," I recited, "symbolizes that 'all truth may be circumscribed into one great whole.' The square represents 'exactness and honor'; the navel mark, 'the need of constant nourishment to body and spirit....'" By now Chris was reciting along with me, "The knee mark, that every knee shall bow and every tongue shall confess that Jesus is the Christ."

Chris was smiling. He understood what I was getting at.

"Right?" I said. "I still believe in all those things. They've got nothing to do with rules or commandments or ordinances. Truth, honor, spiritual nourishment, prayer—that's all between me and our Heavenly Father."

"You know," Chris said, grasping one of my gesticulating arms, "I've never thought about it that way before. But you're absolutely right."

I laughed. "You mean you're just now figuring that out?" I leaned over and kissed him on the back of the neck. "It'll save a lot of time if you just go ahead and agree with me now."

Chris slid off my chest and gave me a playful shove. "Oh, sure, smartass. You'd like that, wouldn't you?"

I flipped over and straddled Chris, pinning his arms to the bed beside his head. Chris pretended to struggle, but the joy in his smile reflected back to me my own feelings of love and gratitude that we had this time together.

"Unless you'd rather fight with me," I said.

"No, that's all right," Chris said. "If it makes you feel better to think you're right, I'm okay with that. I don't have anything to prove."

"Prove?" I said. "You think I've got something to prove?" I lowered my face to within inches of Chris's.

Chris stared back at me with a playful smile and a twinkle in his eye.

For a moment I just hovered, meeting Chris's gaze. I wanted to savor this, to burn it into my memory toward that day when it was long behind us. Slowly I lowered my lips to Chris's and parted them. The kiss was deep and passionate, an exchange of long-pent-up hopes and desires, fears and memories. It was a silent data transfer between our unconscious minds.

At length, I rolled off Chris and collapsed beside him in a loose embrace. I was content. It was enough for now.

CHAPTER 29

WE AWOKE early, grabbed the free breakfast in the hotel lobby, and headed west. We drove across the Willamette Valley toward the Coast Range in silence, both lost in thought. There was so much to say, yet the quiet was comforting. I could feel the bond between us without any words being exchanged. I would steal an occasional look at Chris; Chris would respond with a smile, a squeeze of my hand, or his head on my shoulder. I reveled in our togetherness.

"It's so beautiful out here," I said after a while. "I'd forgotten how green everything was here until I went back to Idaho."

"Yeah. That's one of my favorite things about Oregon. That and the ocean," Chris said.

"I know," I said. "I've only seen the ocean once, back when I was ten years old. It's totally amazing. I can't wait to see it again."

"Me too," Chris said. "And this time I'm goin' in."

"Swimming?" I said with disbelief. "Are you nuts? That water's freezing!"

Chris laughed. "I'm not going to swim laps. I just want to feel it, experience the whole thing, you know?"

"No way," I said, shaking my head. "Not me. I still remember how numb my legs were from just trying to wade in it for a minute."

Chris turned to me. "Pansy."

I punched him in the shoulder. "Hey, watch it. You're lucky I'm driving."

"Just keep your eyes on the road, tough guy."

We drove on to the tunes from my iPod playlist. "So what did you tell your dad?" I asked after we'd gone five or six miles.

Chris gave a weighty sigh. "I told him I needed some time to sort things out, that I'd be doing some traveling before I came home."

I looked at him. "And he was okay with that?"

"What choice did he have? It's not like he could force me to come home."

"Still, I'd expect he'd put a little pressure on…."

"You know, I don't think he really wanted me to come home," Chris said, turning to look at the vineyards we were passing. "I'm an embarrassment to him now. Proof of his failure as a father."

"You know that's not true," I said.

"Do I?" Chris said. His tone was wistful, not angry. "I mean, really, do I? You know the church still believes God didn't make us this way. So if God delivered perfect little spirit-children to him and my mom, then something must have gone wrong after that. That's what my dad believes."

"At least the church is finally starting to acknowledge that it's not something that can be 'fixed.'"

Chris gave a sharp, bitter laugh. "Easy for you to say. Your dad's not a General Authority. Not all of them agree on that, apparently. My dad still thinks it can be prayed away."

I didn't respond. I knew Chris was up against something entirely greater than I was. The Merrills were a family in the spotlight, unlike my own. Chris and I came from different classes of Mormons.

Chris turned to me. "He thinks that *you* did this to me, that you recruited me." He laughed. "I was half tempted to tell him it was me who made the first move."

"And it was a good first move, I'll give you that," I said with a laugh.

Chris laughed too. "Yeah, I'd have to agree."

"So did you mention me?" I asked.

"Oh no," Chris said. "He'd have blown a gasket for sure. Probably would have tried an intervention, or sent some bounty hunters or something."

"I'm that dangerous, am I?"

"No, it's just that he thinks I'm out here working on my repentance. You know, trying to find my way back to the straight and narrow."

I looked at him and smiled. Slowly I shook my head. "No. I don't think you're either straight or narrow."

Chris laughed. "Just remember, it's all your fault. God's anointed one has said so."

IT WAS just past noon when we rolled to a stop outside the Salmon River Market. The GPS said we were in Otis, but it didn't look to me like we were anywhere in particular.

"I need a Coke," I said. "You want anything?"

"I'm good," Chris said. "We're almost there, aren't we?"

"The campground's only about sixty miles, but I figure we'll be stopping to check out some views along the way. I mean, if that's okay. I don't mean to be making all the decisions, it's just that—"

"No, no, that's fine," he said. "I appreciate all the work you've done to make this trip happen. I couldn't exactly get online to do it."

"Yeah, well, now that we're finally here, I thought we could take our time. Do you just want to get lunch somewhere and wait till we set up camp to fix dinner?"

"Yeah, sure." He looked around. "But it doesn't look like there's much to eat here."

"I'll ask inside," I said as I stepped out of the car. The pungent scent of salt air immediately flooded my head with vivid memories of my childhood family vacation. We had definitely reached the ocean.

"The guy says the Otis Café is just a mile up that road there and they have some pretty good burgers," I said when I returned. "You up for that?"

OUR BURGERS came, and we were silent for a while as we dug into them.

"Sucks that they don't have fries here," Chris said. "I could really go for some fries about now."

"I'm okay with chips. Better than soggy fries, in any case."

It took us only minutes to down the burgers and chips. Barely twenty minutes after we arrived, we were back in the Blazer turning north onto the Pacific Coast Scenic Byway. We took several opportunities, as I had suggested, to pull off at state parks and scenic overlooks and get out and stretch our legs. It was after five o'clock when we finally reached Oswald West State Park to set up camp for the evening.

"You sure this is the right place?" Chris asked, looking around the parking lot. "I don't see any campsites."

"Nah, we gotta hike down through those trees." I pointed in the direction of the beach, which wasn't visible beyond the small forest. "The online guide said it's a five-minute walk."

"And we're going to carry everything?"

"If you want dinner and a place to sleep, yes," I teased. "Now help me with this stuff, will you?"

"Hey, wait," Chris said with a laugh. "I thought I was the senior companion."

"Not anymore," I said. "Besides, we alternate being in charge. Today's my day. Tomorrow will be yours."

"Promise?"

"Scout's honor," I said, giving him a three-fingered salute.

The camp setup took us about thirty minutes. "That wasn't too bad, was it?" I said when we had gotten the last of our gear stashed.

"Faster than I expected," Chris admitted as he plopped onto one of the two identical sleeping bags I had bought for the trip. "So when's dinner?"

"You gotta make your own," I said. "Go find a couple of sticks you can sharpen. Not too green."

"What, you mean we're having a weenie roast?"

"As I recall," I said with a grin, "you kinda like my weenie."

"Now, now," Chris chided playfully. "Let's not put dessert ahead of dinner."

While Chris gathered and sharpened the roasting sticks, I pulled an onion and red bell pepper out of the cooler and cut them into pieces. Next I brought out a tray of prewashed button mushrooms and a package of stew meat. Soon we were roasting over the open flame in the fire pit.

"I gotta say, that's the best shish kebab I've ever had while camping," Chris said when the meal was done. "Mainly because it's the *only* one I've had while camping."

"Well, you'd better get used to it," I said. "'Cause there's gonna be a lot more down the road."

"Hey," he said, "let's go check out the beach."

"We'd have to put the fire out," I said.

"That's okay. We can start another one later. C'mon." He grabbed a pan and headed for the nearby water spigot without waiting for my reply.

Twenty minutes later we were on the beach. I immediately removed my shoes and dug my toes into the sand. "Yes," I said with relish. "This was my favorite thing as a kid."

A moment later, Chris had his shoes and socks in hand and was running barefoot toward the water. I ran after him.

"I can't believe all the surfers," I said when we'd stopped at the tide line. "They must be freezing out there."

"Nah, they've all got wetsuits on," Chris said. "See?" He pointed to a couple of guys who'd come out of the water and retreated to a sheltered dune near the tree line. "They're neoprene, so they don't feel the cold at all."

As he spoke, the surfers began removing their wetsuits.

"Do they wear anything underneath those?" I asked. "Like swimsuits?" Chris didn't have to answer, as one of the surfers was already butt naked and drying himself off. Nor did it seem Chris was even going to attempt an answer, as he appeared mesmerized by the sight of the blond guy's near-perfect body.

"Uh, hello-o," I said. "Chris?" I waved a hand in front of his face.

"What?" he said, his defensiveness rising. "I was just looking."

"So I noticed," I teased.

"Oh, like you weren't looking too."

"Well, yeah. I mean it's kinda hard not to notice. But you don't have to be so obvious about it."

"What, like I should go hide in the bushes and sneak a peek?" With that he ran into the surf up to about midcalf. "Aaaaaaaaarrrrr!" he shrieked, whether from exhilaration or the numbing cold it was hard to tell. I assumed it was a little of both.

Chris waved at me to come after him, but I remained where I was, shaking my head. I could barely make out his shouts of "Come on!" over the sound of the surf, but I had no intention of following. I got frostbite just thinking about it.

In a matter of minutes Chris was back at my side, drying his legs. "Tomorrow I go all the way."

CHAPTER 30

"HEY, IT'S almost sunset," I said as we strolled the beach. Most of the surfers had come in and were heading up the trail toward the parking area.

"It should be gorgeous too," Chris said, stopping to pick up a seashell.

"I know," I said. "Let's hike up there to watch it!" I pointed to the tall bluff that defined the north end of the beach. "There's a trail from our campsite. I saw it on the signboard. It's called Cape Falcon."

"I don't know," Chris said. "It looks pretty steep."

"Nah, c'mon. It's only about two miles. We can do that in under an hour."

Chris was right. It *was* steep. But I was also right; we made it in fifty-six minutes. We were exhausted, but it was definitely worth it. The view was spectacular. It went on and on, ending only at the fog bank or the horizon; it was hard to tell where one met the other.

And we had arrived at just the right time. The sun sat just below the fog, but still above the horizon. Its rays emerged from between the two to bathe us in warm orange light. The forest behind us and the entire coastline from north to south took on the auburn glow as well.

"Wow," I said, standing behind Chris and wrapping my arms around him as we took in the view. We were easily more than a hundred feet above the water. "This is so amazing."

"Totally," Chris agreed.

"It's so much more intense in person than in the movies."

"And even better when you're sharing it with someone," Chris added. "I saw a lot of sunsets when I was assigned to the Seaside ward, but they never felt like this." He gave me a quick kiss on the neck.

"There it goes," I said as the red ball of light slid below the water's edge. When it had completely disappeared from view, I turned and put my lips to Chris's. Chris turned toward me and returned the kiss, gently at first and then with increasing passion. I pulled him closer and basked in the joy of having this time with him.

A sound caused us both to disengage. I turned and saw a middle-aged couple emerge from the forest canopy where the trail entered the clearing on the bluff. They approached from about fifty feet away.

Chris pulled away from me and stepped back a couple of feet. I turned to look out over the ocean. I could tell he was embarrassed. The couple arrived at the edge of the bluff a few feet away.

"Hi," I said.

"Hello," the woman said brusquely. Her husband didn't respond.

The four of us stood staring at the view, unmoving, like so many Easter Island statues.

After about a minute, Chris broke the silence. "Well, shall we go?"

When we reached the campsite, we began tidying up, making sure all the food items were securely stored in the cooler. I was pretty sure there were no bears around, but who knew what other nocturnal critters might show up? When we were done, we crawled into the tent and lay atop our sleeping bags, which we had zipped together into one giant bed.

"That was a totally awesome sunset," I said as I pulled Chris to me in a one-armed embrace.

"Yeah, it was," Chris said, snuggling. After a moment he said, "I'm sorry about earlier."

"What do you mean?"

"You know, up on the bluff, when those people saw us kissing. It freaked me a little. I'm not used to being so obvious."

"I know," I said. "It's awkward for me too. But I figure they'll just have to get used to it. I don't want to let the prejudices of others govern how I live my life, so…."

"But sometimes you have to," Chris said, propping himself up on an elbow and looking me in the eye. "There will always be things that, even if they're not wrong, are inappropriate in certain circumstances."

I leaned over and gave him a quick kiss. "Is this private enough for you?"

Before he could respond, I silenced him with another, longer kiss. "Let's get private, then," I said.

CHAPTER 31

DURING OUR companionship and in our letters to each other, Chris and I had often mentioned places we'd like to explore someday: the Pacific Coast, the northern Rockies, Yellowstone, and the Grand Canyon among them. Now that our road trip had become a reality, we had no set itinerary; our only plan was to wake up each morning and decide whether to stay or move on. But we would, in all likelihood, try to include as many of those destinations as possible.

After a week on the Oregon coast—four days at Oswald West and another three farther north at Fort Stevens—we were ready for our next destination. But having endured so many days without a shower, and following Chris's full-body immersion in the salty Pacific, there was no doubt we needed to splurge for a hot shower and laundry facilities. We agreed that once a week was the minimum requirement going forward.

We drove north from Astoria across the mouth of the Columbia River into Washington and began to look for an affordable motel. In Long Beach we found just what we were looking for at Skamania Lodge, a cluster of bungalows just a block from the beach, where a double went for just eighty dollars a night.

When we inquired about laundry facilities, Ken, the owner, told us that while there was no guest Laundromat, we were welcome to use his own washer and dryer by appointment. When he had finished showing us around the property and led us to our bungalow, he added, "And stop by about five thirty if you'd like to join us for happy hour."

"Uh, thanks, but we don't drink," Chris said.

"You must get awfully thirsty, then," Ken said with a wink.

"Alcohol, I mean," Chris added, either missing Ken's humor or purposely ignoring it.

"Well, that's okay," Ken said. "We serve virgins too."

Chris looked shell-shocked.

I cut through the awkwardness. "Right. Those are drinks without alcohol," I said for Chris's benefit.

"Oh yeah," Chris said, clearly embarrassed. "Well, thanks," he said to Ken, moving to the door to show him out.

"That guy was totally flirting with you," I said once we were alone.

"He was not!"

"Oh, come on," I said. "He was so checking you out! Why do you think he walked us over here and spent so much time showing us around?"

"You're jumping to conclusions," he objected. "He's in the tourist industry. It's his job to make people feel at ease."

"And inviting us into his home for happy hour?" I said.

"You think everybody's gay," he said with a laugh. "You think everyone's going around checking out other guys because that's what you're doing."

"Yeah, like you're not," I said.

"Maybe, but I'm not so obvious about it."

"Oh, right. I guess we should ask those surfers about that," I teased.

"Speaking of surf," Chris said, changing the subject, "what do you say we go check out this 'World's Longest Beach' before 'happy hour'?"

"HI, I'M Henry," the man said. "Come on in. Ken's in the kitchen."

"Thanks. I'm RJ."

"And I'm Chris."

Henry shook hands with both of us and led the way into the tiny living room just beyond the motel office. I stole a glance at Chris with a "told you so" raise of the eyebrows. Chris returned the look with a nearly imperceptible shrug.

"Have a seat," Henry said, gesturing toward a love seat in the corner.

Henry seated himself in a chair opposite us. As he did, Ken entered from the kitchen, bearing a tray laden with cheese and crackers and a bowl of mixed nuts. "I hope you two aren't vegan," he said with a laugh as he set the tray on the large ottoman before us. "You said no alcohol; can I get you some coffee?"

"No, we're fine," Chris said. "This is great."

"You have to have something to drink," Ken insisted. "I can mix you up a virgin piña colada or margarita, or if you prefer, I've also got Pepsi, ginger ale, and iced tea. Oh, and I believe we have lemonade too."

"I'm good with ginger ale," Chris said.

"Yeah, same for me," I said.

When Ken had returned with the drinks and finally seated himself, he turned to me. "So, your registration card says you're from Idaho Falls."

"That's my parents' address," I said. I wasn't sure why, but I didn't want to claim it as my home at that moment. There was something liberating about not having to be from anywhere.

"Are you both from Idaho Falls?" Ken asked, gazing at Chris.

"No. I'm from Salt Lake City."

Ken threw a glance at Henry and gave a knowing smile. "Salt Lake City?" he said. "Mormon country."

"Yeah," Chris said. "That it is."

Ken continued the interrogation. "So where did you two meet?"

"Portland," Chris said.

"Oh, I love Portland," Ken said, glancing at Henry again. "We've talked about—you know, when we give up this place—moving to Portland." Turning back to Chris, he asked, "How long were you there?"

"Two years," Chris said.

"I was only there for a few months," I said. "We were just outside Portland, actually. A little place called Clackamas Falls."

"I think we've been through there, haven't we, Henry?" Ken said. He turned back to Chris and me and asked, "So how long have you two been together?"

Well, that's an awkward question, I thought. *Does he mean* together *together? Is he just assuming we're gay?*

When I failed to answer, Ken stared at Chris, who was looking at me. I peeked back at Chris, and we silently wondered which one of us was going to answer the question. "Uh," I stalled, trying to fill the awkward silence. "That's kind of complicated."

"You don't have to answer," Henry interjected. "Ken can get a bit personal sometimes."

"I'm sorry," Ken said. "Henry's right. I don't mean to be nosy, it's just that I love learning about our guests. There are so many interesting people passing through here all the time."

"No, that's okay," I said. I wondered if Chris would be uncomfortable telling these guys the whole story. Ken had, after all, already pegged us as a couple. I looked at Chris for some clue as to how I should answer. I was surprised when Chris took the lead.

"We were assigned as missionary companions six months ago in Clackamas Falls, Oregon."

Ken blushed and began to sputter. "Oh, I'm sorry. I just, well, I assumed…. You see, most of our guests are gay—we advertise in the community papers—so when two men check in together, well…."

Henry stepped in to assist. "We're not used to seeing Mormon missionaries dressed, well, in anything but Sunday attire. We didn't realize that's who you were."

"No, no," Chris responded. "We're not missionaries anymore."

Our hosts looked even more confused.

I couldn't stand it any longer. Only the full explanation could dispel the awkwardness. "We fell in love while we were serving," I explained. "Now that our missions are over, we're on a road trip for a few months before winter semester starts back at school."

It took a moment for what I'd said to sink in, but I saw the lights come on first for Henry, then Ken.

"I'm guessing that's a little unorthodox," Henry said.

"Uh, yeah," I said. "You could say that." I looked at Chris.

"Really unorthodox," Chris said.

"Well, I'm not quite sure what to say," Ken said. "I'm astounded."

"Yeah, well, pretty much everybody is," I said, trying to lighten the conversation. "Especially us."

Chris laughed. "That's true. I sure didn't expect this."

For the next half hour our hosts peppered us with questions about our situation, how the church responded, whether we planned to return to Utah or Idaho, whether we hoped to get married, and so on. When the topic seemed to have been overworked, I felt a need to change the subject.

"So where are you guys from?"

"I'm from Spokane," Henry said, "but spent most of my adult life in Seattle. Ken's from California."

"Marin County," Ken elaborated. "But who can afford to live there anymore? There's no way we could have something like this there."

"So how did you meet?" Chris asked.

"Oh, it's boring, really," Ken said. "Certainly not as interesting as your story."

"We met in a bar in Seattle," Henry said. "I'd been living there working as a staff writer for *Seattle Magazine*. I didn't go out a whole lot, but one night I did, and I met Ken."

"I was there on vacation for the Labor Day weekend," Ken interjected. "It was auspicious timing." He smiled at Henry.

"Maybe it was meant to be," Chris offered.

"It sounds like you had an interesting job," I said to Henry. "What kind of stuff did you write?"

"Mostly arts and entertainment, some travel."

"Sounds like fun," I said. "I've actually thought about becoming a writer."

"Ever done any writing?"

"No, nothing serious. I keep a journal, but that's about it."

"Have you been to college?"

"One year at University of Idaho is all."

"You ought to think about a communications major," Henry said. "If you're truly interested in writing."

"Yeah," I said. "I might look into it when we get back."

"So you're both planning to go back to school?" Ken asked.

Chris shrugged. "Yeah, I mean, that's pretty much a given."

"And what will you study?" Ken asked him.

"I'm not sure. My dad wants me to get an MBA."

Ken's response couldn't have been more on target. "Forgive me for saying so, but perhaps what *you* want might be a better criterion for making such an important decision."

CHAPTER 32

THE COASTAL fog receded behind us as we headed east along the north shore of the Columbia. We'd risen early, shaved for the first time since leaving Clackamas Falls, and showered for the third time in a week. And thanks to Ken and Henry's hospitality, we also had clean clothes that had been laundered for us. Our new friends had also helped us select several worthwhile destinations in the Central Cascades during the coming weeks. Before hitting the road, we each wrote a postcard home and left them with Ken to mail. He didn't charge us for the stamps.

Mount St. Helens was awesome, just as I'd hoped. Though I would have loved to actually walk on the volcano, like people did in Hawaii, I still enjoyed the educational displays and films. Mount Rainier was also impressive. There were some great views of it as we approached it from the freeway, and the lodge was beautiful.

Later we caught the ferry from Tacoma to Vashon Island and spent the night in a tepee at a "ranch hostel" there. It was kind of hokey, but Chris really enjoyed it, which made me happy. I was most in love with Chris in those moments when he totally relaxed and let his guard down. He was like a little kid then, full of excitement and wonder.

The next day we rose at a leisurely hour and caught another ferry, this time to West Seattle. "I've been to Seattle before," Chris said as we stood on the forward observation deck. "But this is the first time I've taken a ferry into the city."

"Are you saying," I said, giving him a peck on the cheek, "that I'm the first 'fairy' you've gone to town with?"

Chris giggled. "Definitely! And you're the only fairy I'm interested in riding," he said with a flirtatious smile. It made me want to rip my clothes off, right there on the bow of the *Kitsap*. I settled instead for a quick slap on the ass.

Chris grabbed my arm and gave me a stern look. "Down, boy!"

After driving off the ferry into West Seattle, we began making our way toward the International District, where we planned to rent two bunks at the youth hostel. Getting there, however, was another story. Seattle at rush hour was overwhelming. I was driving and getting more frustrated by the minute.

The combination of one-way streets and traffic seemed to conspire against me. The route was complicated by the fact that dozens of railroad tracks converged upon the Amtrak station directly across from the hostel. A huge construction project at the station proved entirely unnavigable. Even the GPS was no match for the mess, giving instructions that were either impossible to follow or led us in circles through barely moving traffic. I was getting claustrophobic.

"I'm sorry," I said as I pulled into a pay lot and shut off the engine. We were still blocks from the hostel, and on the opposite side of the tracks from it, but I hadn't been able to get there by any route I had tried. "I can't do this anymore. Besides, I don't think there's any such thing as free parking in downtown Seattle, from what I've seen, so we'll just have to pay."

"Yeah, but it's twenty bucks here," Chris complained. "And the sign says 'Overnight only: no in-and-out privileges.' Don't we want to go out later?"

"Look," I blurted, irritated, "you want to take the car and go find free parking? Fine. I'm done with this shit!" I jumped out, slammed the driver's door, and began retrieving my backpack from the back of the Blazer.

Chris said nothing as he got out and retrieved his pack as well. I was already feeling guilty, but my blood was still boiling from the traffic frustrations. We walked the dozen blocks to the hostel in silence.

As we waited at the light just across the street from the hostel, I spoke. "Look, I'm sorry, okay?" I stared at Chris apologetically. "I'm not used to dealing with this craziness." I swept my hand toward the throngs of cars that seemed to be coming and going from every direction. "I'm a little stressed out right now. I just want to get checked in and go find a quiet place to regain my sanity."

"That's okay," Chris said flatly. "You're entitled."

I could tell he was hurt. I leaned over to give him a kiss, but he reared back out of reach.

"Sorry," I said. "I just wanted to make it up to you."

The light had changed, and Chris was already crossing. When I caught up to him at the far curb, he gave me a tight smile but said nothing.

When we checked in at the hostel—forty dollars per night per person was steeper than we'd expected for a bunk and a communal bathroom—I asked the desk clerk where we might find a quiet place to hang out and decompress for a while. She directed us to the Seattle Center at the opposite end of downtown.

By the time we stepped off the streetcar an hour later, our conversation had returned to normal. Chris seemed to have forgiven my outburst. The last time I'd raised my voice at him was the morning Elder Harris had walked in on us in bed together. That seemed like a lifetime ago already.

The wide open space of the Seattle Center was a relief to both of us. The late-summer sun was still warm, and the cool breeze coming in off the Sound resulted in a perfect temperature.

"So, you want to go up?" Chris asked, indicating the six-hundred-foot Space Needle tower under which we were now standing. "I've been up there before, so it's your call."

"Looks awesome," I said, "but I'd rather save our money and just take a walk instead. We can probably get the same view from up there." I pointed to a bluff above the freeway a mile or so to the east. "I looked at the map. I'm pretty sure that's Capitol Hill, the gay neighborhood Ken and Henry told us about."

CHAPTER 33

"IT DOESN'T look particularly gay to me," Chris said after we'd been walking up Broadway for about ten minutes. "I mean, outside of a few rainbow flags here and there, it looks like every other place I've been."

"What were you expecting? A carnival? Disneyland rides? A 'gay train,' maybe?" I said with a laugh.

"No. But I thought there'd be a bunch of guys holding hands, obvious stuff, you know?"

"Maybe we just haven't gotten to the right part yet."

"But look at this street." He gestured back from where we'd come. "If nobody'd told you it was the 'gay district,' would you have any clue?"

"No," I agreed. "Maybe it's all behind closed doors. Maybe we have to go into some of these places to see it."

"You mean, like bars?" Chris said, his reluctance evident. "'Cause I'm not really comfortable with that. I mean, neither of us drinks. So what would we do there? They'd probably look at us funny if we just ordered root beer."

I laughed. "I bet they don't even have root beer!"

"Maybe if we see some gay people, we can ask," he said with obvious sarcasm.

I laughed again. "Yeah, like, 'Hi. We're brand-new gays. Can you tell us where we go to sign up?'"

Chris laughed too. "I don't think we're any good at this. There probably aren't a lot of gay Mormons."

"You know, I've heard of an organization. I think it's called Affirmation, or something like that. It's nothing but gay Mormons. Returned missionaries, even."

"Well, it can't be very big," he scoffed. "I mean, how many can there be who would do what we did?"

"True," I said. "Most of them are probably in the closet or reparative therapy or something."

"Well, I'm sure they're not here in Seattle. What are the chances?"

"Yeah," I agreed. "You're probably right about that."

We walked on a few more blocks. "Why don't we just find a place for dinner and call it a night?" Chris suggested. "We still have laundry to do, and there are only two washers back at the hostel, so we may have to wait a while."

"Okay. Let's see what looks good."

We walked on. "Ha," I laughed. "There's an old-fashioned drive-in called Dick's—that gay enough for you?"

Chris laughed. "The funny thing is, it looks like it's been here a long time, probably long before this was considered a gay neighborhood."

"Well, it seems to be popular. You want to try it?"

"I don't know," he said, turning up his nose. "I'm all for saving money and all, but as long as we're not camping, I'd like something more than a burger or weenie."

I smiled, but before I could say anything, he added, "And yes, I know—*that* weenie doesn't count."

We walked on, past several sandwich shops and a handful of places that looked too pricey, until it seemed we had been walking for hours. "Hey, there's a sushi place across the street," I suggested.

"That's just raw fish, right?"

"Mostly, I think," I said. "I've never had it. They've probably got something vegetarian without fish too."

"I think that's a bit outside my comfort zone."

"Hey, do you remember why we're here?" I asked.

"In Seattle?"

"On this road trip."

"Well, yeah, I mean—"

"Because Rodney said we needed to get out and experience the world, try new things. Isn't that why we're doing this?"

"I explicitly remember Taco Bell," he said. "I don't recall anything about sushi."

"C'mon," I said with a laugh, taking Chris by the arm and leading him to the crosswalk. "The world is our oyster, even if it *is* raw."

Aoki Sushi Bar turned out to be a more pleasant experience than either of us had expected. When Chris tried to order the teriyaki chicken roll, one of the few items that was cooked and wasn't fish, I protested. "Aw, c'mon. This is supposed to be a new experience. We both have to try something raw."

After a bit of whining, he relented and ordered a salmon roll, reasoning that since he'd had smoked salmon before, he'd already eaten it uncooked and liked it. I went with the spicy California roll, which contained crab and avocado, two foods I already liked.

"Oh wow. Check out those sky colors," Chris said as we were finishing our dinner.

"Nice," I said. "I bet if we hurry we could get a really good view of the sunset farther down the hill, where there aren't so many buildings.

We left the restaurant and headed west down Mercer Street until we were standing at the railing just above the interstate. The sprawling view was bookended to our left by the skyscrapers of downtown and to the right by the rise of Queen Anne Hill. In the flat expanse between stood the Space Needle, like a fishhook plunged into the orange center of the salmon egg that was the sun. It sat poised above the jagged peaks of the Olympic Range, from where, in a last blaze of glory, it scorched the undersides of the scattered clouds that floated above Puget Sound.

"That is so awesome," I said. "I could totally live here, couldn't you?"

"I don't know," he said, surreptitiously taking my hand in a rare public display. "I mean, it's beautiful as far as cities go, but I kind of need the mountains."

"There are mountains here. Look, right over there." I pointed to the Olympics in the distance. "They're not the Tetons, but they're as good as the Wasatch Front—better, even, 'cause these are right on the ocean."

"But they're too far away," he objected. "I want 'em right here, close enough to touch, like at home. I want to hike up the canyons."

I regarded Chris for a long moment. "You miss Salt Lake, don't you?"

"Well, yeah," he said. "I mean…." He looked away.

"Your family?"

Chris nodded. When he turned to speak, I saw his eyes had moistened. "You know, they're not bad people, RJ. They just don't understand this," he said, indicating our joined hands.

"I know," I said. "It's the same with my parents. That's why I needed this time away. Heck, I think they needed it more than I did. It was pretty intense there right after I got sent home."

"Yeah. Well, at least that's behind you now. My day of reckoning is still hanging over my head."

As the toothy grin of the Olympics swallowed the last of the sun's rays, I leaned over and gave Chris a kiss. "So do you want to walk back to the hostel, or should we try to figure out the bus system?"

"I'm good for a walk. Which way?"

CHAPTER 34

"HEY, YOU know what? I think this is a gay bar," I said as we passed a doorway in front of which a long line of people stretched up the sidewalk from behind a rope line. "Check out some of these guys."

"Yeah," Chris agreed. "I think you're right."

"Hey," I said, stopping and turning to Chris. "Let's go in."

Before Chris could veto the suggestion, I added, "Remember Rodney!"

He laughed and shook his head. "Is that going to be your rallying cry from now on?"

"If it works," I said playfully.

"Well, Rodney also said we needed to get drunk and spend a night in jail, and I have no intention of doing either of those things."

"Oh come on, just for a few minutes," I cajoled. "I mean, we're here, there's no pressure, no schedule. When is there going to be a better time?"

Chris screwed up his face. I could tell his defenses were crumbling.

"C'mon, let's get in line."

As we walked back down the block, it was hard not to notice how many really good-looking guys there were. I could see Chris was checking them out too. I took his hand when we reached the end of the line. Chris gave me a quick smile but said nothing. He stood stiffly, looking uncomfortable.

"Hey, don't worry," I said, squeezing his hand. "It'll be fun."

When we reached the front of the line, the bouncers did more than just check our IDs. They looked us up and down as though they were buying a couple of horses. It made me uncomfortable. We apparently passed the visual inspection, because they let us in.

The Lobby was definitely more hip than any of the restaurant bars I had seen back home, which were the only bars I'd ever peeked into before. This place was retro and gaudy, like something from an

Austin Powers movie. I supposed it was meant to be stylish, but it was kind of over-the-top.

Chris's gaze darted nervously around the room. I sensed it was not the décor that had caught his attention but the mass of good-looking men. All of them seemed to be fit, trim, and under thirty. Most were wearing sport shirts and slacks or jeans. A few wore T-shirts stretched tight as a coat of paint applied to their bulging pecs and rippling abs. There didn't seem to be an ounce of extra fat on any of them.

I took Chris by the hand and led him wordlessly to a free table near the back. The music was loud, and we had to half shout to be heard above it. "So what do you think?" I asked after we'd sat down.

He just raised his eyebrows. He seemed overwhelmed.

"I know, right? These guys all look like models."

We'd been silently surveying the crowd for a few minutes when a good-looking waiter who looked even younger than we did appeared out of nowhere. "What can I get you?" he asked, looking from one to the other of us. He didn't smile and seemed to be in a hurry.

Chris was tongue-tied, so I answered for both of us. "Do you have Sprite?"

The waiter looked at me impassively. "Yeah."

"Okay," I said. "Can we get two, please?"

He disappeared into the crowd without acknowledging the order.

"He probably thinks we're twelve years old," Chris said. "Just drinking pop." He laughed. "To tell the truth, he's so skinny he doesn't look much older than twelve himself."

"I think he's giving us attitude because we're not big spenders."

"Well, I hope he doesn't expect a tip. He could have at least smiled."

We turned our attention to the room again, which continued to get more crowded. "You know, this reminds me of a church social," I said. "Except for the alcohol, of course."

Chris laughed. "That, and there's definitely a lot fewer girls."

"Yeah, but more than I expected. And they don't look like lesbians."

"I'm not sure I'd know what a lesbian looks like," he said. "I mean, unless she's making out with another lesbian."

"You know what I mean," I said. "Most of these girls look pretty feminine to me. Like, look at those two over there." I gestured with my chin. "The one on the left is hanging on to that guy. They look like a straight couple."

"True. I suppose straight people could come in here without knowing it's a gay bar. I mean, there's nothing on the sign that says 'gay bar.' We just assumed because of all the hot guys."

"Heck, maybe we were the idiots. Maybe it's not even a gay bar!" I laughed. "I don't see any guys making out anywhere."

"Either way, it's a bar. And it's the first time I've been in one," Chris said.

"It's not bad, is it?" I asked. "I mean, this music's pretty good. I could even dance to it."

"Yeah. I actually miss church dances. I mean, after two years a guy needs to cut loose, you know?" Chris laughed and pantomimed a dance move in his chair.

"It is." The voice came from the next table. We both turned toward the source: a slender, handsome guy who was sitting alone. He had short, dark hair and the barest hint of a mustache.

"Excuse me?" I said.

"This *is* a gay bar," the guy said.

"Ah, well, thanks," I said, glancing at Chris.

An awkward silence fell. I didn't feel like continuing the conversation, and if I carried on with Chris, then this guy would be listening in.

"There's dancing upstairs," the guy said, pointing upward.

"Oh, really?" I said. I didn't want to seem impolite, but it was kind of rude of him to be eavesdropping. "Well, thanks. Maybe we'll check it out."

The guy smiled. "The stairs are over there," he said, indicating the back of the room.

"Okay. Great," I said, returning a quick smile. I turned back to Chris. "So you want to go check it out?"

"I don't know," Chris said. "I'm kind of okay here. You can go if you want."

"I'd rather we both go." I used my eyes to indicate our eavesdropper.

Just then the waiter arrived with our Sprites. "Did you want to open a tab?"

I was confused. "Uh, Tab? No, thanks, just the Sprites."

The waiter rolled his eyes dramatically. "Seven dollars."

I reached into my pocket, but Chris stopped me. "No, it's my turn to pay." He pulled out a ten and handed it to the waiter.

"Thanks," I said with a smile.

Once the waiter had handed Chris his change and disappeared, I lobbied again to go upstairs. "It won't hurt to go look. C'mon."

"No, that's okay," Chris demurred again. "Really, go on if you want."

I laughed nervously. "Actually, I'm kind of scared," I confessed.

"I'll go with you." It was the guy at the next table again. "C'mon. I'll show you the way." He was already on his feet at my side.

I looked from the guy to Chris and back again, hesitating.

"I was about to head up there anyway," the guy said. He stuck out his hand toward Chris. "Hi. My name is Paul."

Chris shook the hand as though it might be contaminated. "Chris."

Paul then offered his hand to me.

"Uh, hi. I'm RJ."

"Well, RJ, I'm on my way up, so if you care to join me...." Paul sauntered toward the stairs, pausing to look back.

I looked at Chris and shrugged. I turned back to Paul. "Okay, just for a few minutes, I guess." I threw Chris a smile and trotted off toward the stairs.

"After you," Paul said with an outstretched hand.

The music was incredibly loud. Paul pulled up to my side and practically shouted in my ear. "The dance floor doesn't really get crowded until about ten o'clock. But I like to come earlier. I'm kind of claustrophobic."

I nodded an acknowledgment and smiled. It seemed pointless to try to say anything. Paul and I walked to the edge of the dance floor, where only seven people, all men, were rocking out to a heavy beat: three couples and one guy by himself.

"So, I'm guessing you and your friend are new in town," Paul said. The sound level practically required him to put his mouth on my ear.

It made me shiver. The only mouth I'd ever had on my ear was Chris's, and the gesture sent my mind to more private places. "Uh, yeah," I said. "We're actually only here for tonight."

Paul shook his head and pointed to his own ear, turning it to me. I leaned in as Paul had done a moment earlier and repeated my answer. I stopped short of actually putting my lips on his ear.

"You on a layover?" Paul asked.

"Kind of. I mean, we're driving, not flying. We're on a road trip."

Paul's eyebrows lifted. "You drove to Seattle to spend only one night here?"

"It's a camping trip, really," I explained. "We just came into the city to do our weekly laundry."

Paul laughed. His dimples were deep and expressive. "I think you've come to the wrong place." He looked around conspicuously. "The only agitators I see are those guys twerking out there," he said, nodding toward the dance floor.

I laughed too. Maybe I had misjudged Paul. He was funny and easygoing, and kind of cute too. "Yeah, well, we're doing the laundry at the international hostel. But we thought we'd take a look around as long as we were here. We're heading out to North Cascades National Park tomorrow."

"Awesome place," Paul said. "I was just there in June."

"Really? Maybe you can recommend a good camping spot."

"Sure. In fact, I've got pictures." Paul pulled out a mobile phone and started poking at it. "Here. Check this out." He squeezed in tight so we could both see the tiny display.

I could smell his deodorant, or maybe it was his shampoo. It was a pleasant fragrance. It was totally unintentional, but I felt myself getting an erection. The warmth of Paul's shoulder up against my own, and the citrus-alcohol scent of his breath when he spoke, made my heart race.

"This is Goodell Creek. It's an awesome place to camp," Paul was saying. "Quiet, beautiful. Most people go to the Newhalem Campground just up the road, so there's lots of privacy." He turned and smiled at me.

I was too unnerved to take in all that Paul was saying. The physical sensation I was experiencing was at odds with my feelings for Chris. I wasn't looking for another guy; I hadn't been seeking sexual thrills. But there it was, a physical and emotional response to a complete stranger. Why? Because of his scent? His smile? Why couldn't I control this? I loved Chris!

I searched for an excuse to disengage, but before I found it, one presented itself. Chris was standing next to me. So immersed had I been in Paul's allure that I hadn't even seen Chris approach. "Oh, hey," I said with exaggerated enthusiasm, immediately pulling away from Paul and his phone. "I didn't see you there."

"Obviously," Chris said tersely.

"Hey," Paul said, putting his phone away. But Chris did not return the greeting.

"Paul was just showing me some great camping spots we might check out tomorrow night."

"How nice," Chris said with obvious sarcasm. "Will he be joining us?"

CHAPTER 35

"NOTHING WAS going on, Chris." I said again. "Why won't you believe me?"

"So that's why he gave you his phone number, I suppose." We were halfway back to the hostel already and still Chris refused to look at me. In fact, this was his first response since we'd left the bar.

"He gave *us* his card," I emphasized. "You were there too. It's just a common courtesy, nothing more."

But Chris remained unswayed. He said nothing more until we reached the hostel. Even then he kept his verbal communications to a bare minimum until we were bedded down in our separate bunks. His silence spoke volumes, however.

I lay in bed, staring at the ceiling. Had I done something wrong? I wasn't sure. Maybe Chris did have reason to be jealous. I had been, after all, sporting a hard-on while standing shoulder to shoulder with a cute guy. Chris had noticed. That didn't look so good, I had to admit. But it was entirely unintentional; I'd tried to explain that to Chris. The guy was just showing me some vacation pictures. That was all there was to it. I couldn't control my erections. What guy could?

My excuses got no traction with Chris, though. Maybe he'd be more reasonable in the morning. I rolled onto my side and pulled the sleeping bag close around my neck. But sleep eluded me. Unfortunately, the erection did not; it remained constant. I did not want to think of Paul. I forced the encounter from my mind, choosing instead to think only of Chris. The result was a melancholy mix of passion and heartache that just made me more miserable.

I must have dozed off eventually, because it was suddenly morning. That was a mixed blessing. On the one hand, I could finally get busy and stop replaying the previous night in my mind. On the other, I was so exhausted from lack of sleep that I was functioning on autopilot.

"I think you'll have to do the driving today," I told Chris over breakfast. "I didn't sleep a wink."

Chris continued to eat his toast in silence.

"Is that okay?" I prodded.

"Yeah." He still refused to look me in the eye.

Chris's coldness was killing me. I had tried explaining and apologizing the night before, and that hadn't worked. Now I was forcing myself to just act normally, like nothing was wrong.

After breakfast we did the laundry largely in silence. We wrote our weekly postcards home in silence, then headed out to the grocery store, a similarly quiet affair. I picked out the food, and Chris occasionally shrugged his approval or grunted his disapproval. We were finally on the road northward just after noon, with Chris behind the wheel. I thought I might be able to get some sleep, but the tension between us weighed too heavily to let me relax.

"Look," I said about thirty minutes into the drive, "I know what it looked like. But I swear to you I was not interested in that guy. We were making polite conversation. I mentioned North Cascades, and he whipped out his phone and started showing me pictures. That's it." I looked at him imploringly. "Really. Okay?"

Chris licked his lips before speaking, but he kept his eyes on the road. "I'm sorry. I overreacted, I know." He stole a glance at me, the first sympathetic look I had seen since the incident. I smiled, relieved. He smiled back, then returned his eyes to the road.

We exited the freeway at Woodinville to pick up State Route 9 to Snohomish. "You know," he said as we waited at a stoplight, "I'm totally new at this." He looked me in the eye, his own eyes brimming with tears. His voice broke as he continued. "I've never been in love before." The light changed. He wiped his eyes and returned his attention to the road. "It's so beautiful at times. But it's also really scary."

"I know," I said. "It is." I gave Chris a smile of encouragement. "And this is totally new to me too. I mean, when I told you I'd been intimate with men before—just that one time—it was only physical, never like this."

"You see," he said, "that's what scares me. I know there are a lot of guys out there who are a lot cuter than me."

"No," I said, cutting him off. "Don't even think that way."

"But it's true."

"Chris, I didn't fall in love with you because of your looks."

"Gee, thanks," he said. "That makes me feel a whole lot better."

"Wait, wait, wait!" I spluttered. "That totally came out wrong!" He laughed.

"You know what I mean," I said. "I love you for who you are, for what we've shared. Of course you're good-looking. But that's beside the point—that's what I meant."

He shot me a smile. "Well, that's better, I guess."

"Look," I said in all seriousness, "there will always be better-looking guys than both of us. If we go around comparing, we'll always be insecure. We just can't do that."

"But it's hard not to notice."

"Well, yeah," I conceded. "I mean, you can't not see them. But you can't go around avoiding them either."

Chris appeared to think about that but said nothing.

"If we're going to have a relationship, it's got to be built on trust." I looked at him. "I want you to trust me, Chris."

"I do," he protested, but then he added, "well, I guess maybe I didn't last night. But that's me, not you."

"It's hard, I know," I acknowledged. "If the tables were reversed last night, I probably would have gotten jealous too. I really don't blame you." I leaned over and gave him a peck on the cheek. "So are we done fighting?"

"Yeah."

"Good. Because I feel like we have an amazing day ahead of us."

An hour and a half later we had reached the national park and found the campground Paul had recommended. There was only one available campsite remaining. It wasn't as private as we'd hoped, but at least it was right on the Skagit River. We set up camp, cooked burgers over the campfire, and sat out under the stars talking until I began to fade.

"I'm sorry, but I'm going to have to call it a night," I told Chris shortly before nine o'clock. "I hardly slept at all last night."

"Yeah, neither did I."

"Wait, what? I let you drive all day! Why didn't you say something?"

"One of us had to drive," Chris said with a shrug. "I didn't mind."

I shook my head. "Some road-trippers we are. What do you say next time we fight, we make up before we go to bed so we can get some sleep?"

"I don't know," Chris said with an impish grin. "If we make up before hitting the sack, we still may keep each other up all night."

I laughed. "You have a point there. But don't even think of sex tonight. I can barely keep my eyes open."

When I awoke, the sun was lighting the tips of the peaks to the west. Chris was already up and fixing breakfast. After we'd eaten, we sat down to examine the park map and plan the day ahead.

"This looks like it'd be an awesome hike," I said, pointing to a route labeled Thurston Lakes Trail.

Chris leaned in and examined to where I was pointing. "Definitely a good workout. Look, the trailhead's at 2,900 feet and it climbs to 5,000 feet. And it's five miles one way." Then, spotting another map feature, he pointed. "Ha! Damnation Creek. That's fitting, don't you think?"

"Well, I wouldn't take it too personally. From the names of the peaks around here—Mount Terror, Mount Despair, Mount Fury—I'd say the folks who named this place generally weren't very optimistic."

An hour later we parked at the trailhead and began our climb. It was easy going for the first couple of miles. The trail gained only a couple hundred feet as it ascended a wash, crossed Thornton Creek, and switched back along the opposite slope. But then it began to climb steeply through a dense old-growth forest.

Four hours after we began, we stood at a fork atop the trail's summit, looking down upon a cluster of tiny—but obviously deep—alpine lakes.

"Wow," Chris said. "This was definitely worth it."

"Absolutely," I agreed, pulling out my phone to snap some pictures. "Look at the color of that water. That's amazing." I gave Chris a kiss. "Get over here and let's get a shot of both of us." I put my arm around Chris, pulled him close, and snapped a selfie against the background of jagged alpine peaks.

"You ready to head down to the lake?" I asked, pocketing my camera.

"I don't know," Chris said with a heavy sigh. "It's pretty steep. We'd have to climb back up."

"Aw, c'mon," I prodded. "It's only another half mile."

"Yeah, but it's also about a five-hundred-foot descent," Chris complained. "I don't know if I've got it in me. I'm pretty out of shape."

"What are you talking about? You run every day. Don't be a wimp. We'll have lunch at the bottom, then rest up until we're ready to tackle the return."

WE AROSE early the next morning, mailed postcards to Rodney and our respective families after breakfast, and were soon eastbound on State Road 20. We grabbed lunch in Okanogan and continued on to Sandpoint, Idaho, on Lake Pend Oreille, where we shelled out sixty-eight dollars for a one-star motel. After a whole day of driving, it didn't take me long to fall asleep, but I relished the few waking minutes I spent wrapped tightly in Chris's arms before I did.

Two days later we arrived in Glacier National Park. "You know, I'm loving this trip and all," Chris said as we snuggled in the tent on our first night there, "being here with you." He stopped to cup my face in his hand and kissed me on the forehead. "But," he continued, "I'm kinda getting tired of the driving thing. You know, setting up, packing up, driving, day after day."

"I know. Me too," I agreed. I'd been doing most of the driving, and as much as I enjoyed it, it was losing its magic after two straight weeks of it.

"What do you say we don't go anywhere for the next couple of weeks? Stay right here," Chris said. "There's plenty to see—it's a huge park. And it's not really that cold at night."

"Yet," I added. "We'd planned to be farther south by the end of September, remember?"

"Well, yeah. But let's just wait and see. If it gets too cold, then we can move on, right?"

"Sure. I could hang here for a couple of weeks. We're in no hurry, and we've got a great camping spot."

The sex that night was the best it had ever been, and I was pretty sure Chris would agree with my assessment. The romance of the remote and rugged landscape surrounding us brought out something primal and visceral in us. On the one hand, our lovemaking felt almost animalistic in its carnality. Yet it was also full of tenderness and spirituality. We spent as much time probing each other's souls as we did our respective bodies. And it was followed by the most restful sleep I could remember having since before my mission. And it wasn't just a one-time thing. The next two weeks at Glacier were magical for me.

One night as we snuggled by the campfire, I expressed those sentiments to Chris. "I think the church is wrong about this," I said. "If the Spirit has not been present in our relationship, then I don't know what the Spirit is. I mean, how can I claim to have a testimony of anything if I have completely mistaken what it is to feel God's presence?"

He stared into the fire and continued to stroke my thigh, but he didn't respond.

"What do you think?" I prompted.

"I don't know," he said, hesitant. "I mean, I think it's a slippery slope to declare the church wrong because of our emotional experiences." He tossed a pinecone into the fire. "And I don't just mean the gay thing."

"But the effects of the Spirit *are* emotional, Chris. Doesn't it make you cry to feel its presence? It does for most people."

"Well, yeah, but a rectangle's not a square. The Spirit may bring on tears, but not every crying fit is a spiritual experience. My mother cried when my father bought her a new Escalade for Mother's Day, but I don't think that means it came from God."

"You're completely missing my point, though. When I read the Book of Mormon and prayed about it before my mission, I got that burning in my heart that we're promised, that confirmation of the Spirit that assures us that it is good, that it's true."

"Right," he agreed. "That's what Moroni promises."

"Right. And that's an extremely emotional experience. It brings tears to your eyes, right? So you can't discount emotions as an expression of a spiritual witness."

"I'm not. I'm just saying that it's dangerous to assume that you know better than the prophets and apostles simply because you had an emotional experience that made you cry."

"Okay, look," I said, getting frustrated. "Let's stop talking in the abstract here. When you and I make love, I feel a very deep emotional and spiritual connection, not only to you, but to our Heavenly Father. I literally thank him for bringing you into my life and letting me share myself fully with you. The burning in my heart is the same burning that confirmed the truth of the Book of Mormon to me."

Chris bit his lip but said nothing. I knew what that meant: he was fighting back tears.

I embraced him and buried my face in his neck. "You see," I said softly. "I know you feel it too. I can feel you feeling it when we make love."

Chris cried softly, and I didn't press the issue any further. I knew he had a much harder time expressing anything critical about the church than I did. Chris would rather take all the blame himself for the things he couldn't reconcile between his own experience and what he'd been taught. Yet another artifact from growing up a General Authority's son.

CHAPTER 36

THE NIGHTS did finally begin to get cold as September wore on, but never were we uncomfortable. We would just wear more layers in the evening and hold each other closer at night. In fact, the favorite part of my day was when we climbed into our conjoined sleeping bags and spooned.

I didn't think it was my imagination that sex was becoming better between us since we had that discussion around the campfire. I'd always sensed that Chris's guilt and internalized homophobia were in the bed with us, but lately Chris had seemed to be more open or more joyful somehow when we made love. Maybe he was coming around to understand what I had been talking about; maybe he was finally allowing himself to feel the Spirit in the way I had.

I too was learning as our sexual relationship matured. My insecurities and performance anxiety began to lessen with practice, and we both learned to slow down and savor the experience. Focusing less on the mechanics of sex allowed me to feel more of a oneness with Chris, not only while we were in the throes of passion, but afterward as well. It made even our disagreements easier to bear, because when we got mad at each other, that underlying bond was still there through it all.

I thought of the scripture that said "a man… shall cleave unto his wife, and the twain shall be one." That was exactly what Chris and I were experiencing. Of course, the church would never consider us to be married, even if we went to a state where such a thing was possible. But neither could the church take away what Chris and I had. It could deny that our bond existed, but I knew better. I had a testimony of the Spirit: God had blessed our union.

It was storming the day we arrived in West Yellowstone; fall had definitely arrived in the Rockies. But rather than get us down, the thunder and lightning enhanced the beauty of our surroundings, making the setting more romantic. Still, such weather made camping hazardous, if not entirely impossible. The ranger at the entrance gate advised us to avoid open spaces until the storm advisory had passed, and not to set up our tents under lone or small clusters of trees, even if it was drier there.

"What do you think?" I asked Chris. "It could get pretty hairy out there if this keeps up."

"I don't know," Chris said, looking out at the massive thunderheads in the distance. "What's the alternative? Rooms here in town, if there are even any available, are going to be pretty pricey."

"We could head down the road and get a cheap motel while we wait out the storm. These things don't usually last more than a day or two," I said, pulling out my phone to search. "Here's one— the Guesthouse Inn in Saint Anthony—for only fifty-nine dollars, plus tax."

"How far is that?"

"About an hour south," I said. "But we're in no hurry, right?"

The Guesthouse Inn looked decent enough; it was rated two stars and had auto-club approval. When we went to check in, we found the pricing to be higher than expected.

"I'm sorry," the college-age girl behind the desk told us politely, "that rate is for a single. For two queens it will be seventy-two dollars."

Chris and I stole a glance, and we both burst out laughing. The girl gave us a puzzled look.

"I'm sorry," I said, regaining my composure. "Never mind us. We've just had a very long day."

"For a minute there I thought she had us pegged," Chris said with a laugh when we got outside.

"I know, right? For *you two* queens, that'll be seventy-two dollars!"

"YOU KNOW, I'm only forty miles from home right now," I said as we lay on the bed, flipping aimlessly through TV channels.

"How does that feel?"

"Weird. I mean, it's the only home I've ever known, outside of those few months in Clackamas Falls, but it doesn't feel like it's mine anymore." I kissed Chris on the cheek. "I feel more at home with you, even being on the road."

"I know what you're saying," Chris said, intertwining his fingers with mine. "In some ways Salt Lake feels like it's some distant planet. It's so different from Portland and everything else I've experienced lately."

"But you miss your family, right?"

"Well, yeah. Especially my mom and my sister and brother. I wish I could talk to them."

I reached over and picked up my phone from the nightstand. "You can if you want," I said, holding it out toward Chris.

"Thanks, but no. It would make things awkward for my mom."

"How so?"

"It would put her in between me and my dad, for one. He'd expect her to try to convince me to come home, and she'd lay her own guilt trip on me for making her worry. Then she'd feel obligated to tell me how my dad feels about what I'm doing, and I don't really want to hear it right now. I'll get enough of that when I get home."

"Yeah," I said, putting the phone down, "I totally get it. As much as I love my parents, I need this break. If there's any real emergency, my mom has my number." After a pause I said, "It's six o'clock. What do you say we go find some dinner before this town closes for the night?"

In the end, two days passed before we returned to the park and set up camp. Then we spent nearly three weeks probing every corner of the park, as the weather permitted. Our days alternated between leisurely visits to popular sites, and long hikes into remote areas that were seldom visited. I thought of those places as our own Garden of Eden.

It was already early October when we finally moved on to Grand Teton National Park. It was every bit as magnificent as I remembered from my last visit there at the age of fourteen with the Boy Scouts. Chris was in awe as well.

"I can't believe your family never came here," I said. "It's not that far from Salt Lake."

"Yeah," Chris said. "But my dad's a workaholic. He pretty much hated family vacations. And road trips were the worst. He had no patience for the fights my brother Greg and I would get into in the backseat. I think he'd have been just as happy if he could have skipped vacations altogether." He laughed. "And then, when he was called to the Quorum of the Seventy, forget it. We never went anywhere. In fact, we hardly ever saw him anymore. He was always at a church meeting or traveling to some distant stake to preside over a conference or something."

WEEKS TURNED into months as the days got shorter and colder. We continued east as far as Mount Rushmore, then south through Colorado, visiting Rocky Mountain National Park, saw the first snows of the season in Aspen, and on to Four Corners in search of warmer weather. We spent time on a Navajo reservation and explored the ruins of Canyon de Chelly. We toured New Mexico's Sangre de Cristo Mountains, saw Taos and Santa Fe, and camped on the Rio Grande.

It was the happiest I had ever been. Standing on the rim of the Grand Canyon, my arm around Chris, I was on top of the world. And the world was beautiful. Chris was beautiful. Our love for each other was beautiful.

But I knew all along it wasn't the real world, and that began to weigh heavily on me. The journey had to end soon. We had agreed to return to our families by Thanksgiving and face what consequences would come. We both hoped the holiday season would soften the hearts of our respective fathers and that arguments could be kept to a minimum.

"So, you ready for Utah?" I asked Chris a few days later as we surveyed the endless vista of Monument Valley at sunset.

"Yeah," he said with a heavy sigh. "I've been psyching myself up for it."

"We still have one more month," I reminded him, "and there's lots of awesome country to explore between here and Salt Lake."

"Absolutely," he said. "Now it's my turn to show you *my* favorite places."

I stole a quick peck on the cheek. We were both well aware that public displays of affection would not be permissible during the coming month in Utah.

"I love you," I whispered into his ear.

He turned and looked into my eyes, our faces just inches apart. "I love you too."

We stood unmoving in that spot, arms around each other's shoulders, until the sun set completely.

CHAPTER 37

THE FALL weather began to make camping gradually less comfortable as October rolled on into November. Still, we managed to keep motel stays to one per week as we zigzagged our way northward through Utah. A week split between Zion and Bryce, another between Capitol Reef and Natural Bridges, and a week each in Canyonlands and Arches National Park.

The beauty was stunning. I had never felt more spiritual in my life than standing, sitting, or cuddling with Chris, silently taking in sunrises and sunsets, day after day, in some of the most beautiful places I'd ever seen.

But the time had finally come to face the inevitable return to the lives we had put on hold for nearly four months. Tomorrow we would leave Moab for Salt Lake City. Thanksgiving was four days away. We had not spoken to our families since hitting the road at the end of July; the postcards had been our only communication. We both mentioned each other by name in those cards but said nothing of the deep bond we had been developing. That would soon change.

"You know, I can't help but look at this landscape, with all its gnarly rock formations and ginormous cliffs, and feel like I'm in the Land of Mordor," I said as we shared our last sunset in Arches National Park.

"Ha! Yeah," he said. "And just beyond the horizon"—he pointed northward—"the evil Eye of Sauron sits in Salt Lake City!"

"Luring us closer, waiting to destroy us!" I added. The metaphor was all too accurate. I knew there were forces ahead that would do everything possible to separate us.

"So, which one of us is Frodo?" he asked with an eyebrow raised.

"Definitely you," I said. "I am but your humble servant, Samwise Gamgee."

"No, no. It's got to be you. You've been leading this adventure. I'm just along for the ride."

"I don't know," I said, brushing back his hair, which now nearly covered his ears—neither of us had gotten a haircut since the journey began. "I think you're the one with the ring around your neck. I mean, I don't think I'm likely to be climbing to the top of the church office building and hurling myself onto the temple spires in despair."

"Yeah, but if you did, I'd save you," Chris said. He leaned in and kissed me. I responded, and we savored the kiss for nearly a minute. We continued to sit in a tight embrace, silently watching the last of the sun as it slipped below the horizon, bringing to a close the last full day of the fantasy that had first hatched in Rodney's apartment so long ago.

The November air was chill, and snow already sat upon the higher elevations. Temperatures dropped quickly after sunset, so we wasted no time in retreating to the car. I let Chris drive, since a long day of driving awaited me in the morning.

"So what are you going to tell them?" I asked as we made our way back to the motel in Moab.

"About what?"

"About us."

Chris didn't respond right away. He pursed his lips in thought. "I don't know. I mean, I guess I'm just going to say that we love each other. But only if they ask."

"Chris, I don't really think they're going to ask if you love me. They don't even think such a thing is possible."

"Well, yeah, but they already know about the sex part—on the mission, at least. So when that comes up—'cause you know the bishop's going to ask—I want to put it in the right context."

"That's not a fun conversation, believe me. Church leaders don't want to hear about 'context.' You know, 'when the prophet has spoken, the thinking has been done.' I told my bishop as little as possible," I said.

We continued in silence for a while. "Do you think they'll convene a court for you?" I asked.

"I don't know," Chris said. "It's possible. But I have to think that if they let me finish my mission just so my father wouldn't be embarrassed, then they might just want to sweep it under the rug.

Especially when I tell them I'm transferring to Boise State in the spring. They might just be glad to have me go away quietly."

"Are you really going to do it?" I asked. "Are you going to transfer to Boise State with me?"

"Of course I am," he said. I felt reassured.

"I can't wait until we're there," I said. "I'm ready to get back to school. And it'll be so awesome to share an apartment with you again."

"Yeah," Chris said with a laugh. "It'll be just like the mission."

"With nicer clothes." We both laughed.

"And no reports to Elder Harris!" Chris added.

"Elder Harris," I said, shaking my head. "What a little prick."

"I don't know," he said. "I mean, what would you have done in his shoes? Wouldn't you have gone to the mission president too?"

"Well, yeah, probably. But Harris was such a soulless geek to begin with. It was like he was... I don't know... not human."

"Maybe he's an orc!"

I laughed. "Oh my gosh, you're totally right. He probably keeps a mountain troll in his basement!"

We both laughed again.

"I wonder where he is now," I said.

"I heard he was engaged."

"No! Oh, that poor girl."

"You know she's got a sweet spirit and a burning testimony, right?" Chris said in mock seriousness.

"Totally."

We made love twice that night. I couldn't help but think of those movies where the condemned prisoner gets to order his last meal. I felt like Chris was that meal, to be savored and enjoyed in a way that would sear the experience into my memory. It would have to get me by for the six weeks until the spring term started.

When we had finished for the second time, I lay sprawled on my back, spent. I had a kind of buzz that reminded me of being stoned. It was a happy, euphoric feeling but tinged with a gnawing paranoia. I kept thinking I should do something, something more to take advantage of my last night with him. Yet at the same time, I felt paralyzed, as though I couldn't even move if the room were on fire.

Chris lay beside me. "You know, if they do excommunicate me," he said at length, still staring up at the ceiling, "it'll have one advantage."

"What's that?"

"I'll be able to get some sexier underwear."

"Hey, I think you're plenty sexy in your garments."

"Well, it does make it feel naughtier, that's for sure," Chris said with a laugh.

"So then it's hotter, right?"

"I guess so," Chris said. "Do you plan to keep wearing yours?"

"I don't know," I said. I thought about it. "I guess part of it's political in a way. If I take off the garments, then they've won; they've taken away everything that was ever important to me. I don't want to give them that power. And in a way, the garments are a comfortable reminder of my own spirituality."

"I know what you mean."

"On the other hand," I continued, "they're also a reminder that the plan of salvation as the church has described it doesn't have room for us. You know, the covenant not to have sexual relations 'except with your wife, to whom you are legally and lawfully wedded.'"

"Yeah, there's that," Chris acknowledged. "I think we're pretty much screwed if that's the only option."

I rolled over to face him. "Screw? Did somebody say 'screw'?" I wiggled my eyebrows at him.

"You can't be serious!"

"I am," I said, flipping over on top of him and pinning his arms back beside his head. "I'm very serious."

CHAPTER 38

THE MORNING began quietly: a largely silent breakfast, followed by a load of laundry before checking out of the motel at noon. We grabbed a couple of burgers on our way out of Moab and listened to the radio until the signal became too weak. Neither of us spoke of the heaviness in the air. We didn't need to. Our thoughts were already intertwined.

When we reached Price, the halfway point of our four-hour journey, Chris offered to take the wheel, but I declined. I enjoyed the trancelike state the two-lane highway induced. It helped me focus my thoughts. And there were so many going through my head at that moment.

"You know," I said, "I'm going to write you every week, just like in the mission field."

"You mean, like a pen-on-paper kind of thing?"

"Yeah. It's more personal than e-mail. I think it's romantic. It gives you something tangible you can hold on to and save."

"That's sweet," he said, reaching over and squeezing my thigh.

"Will you write me back? A real letter too?"

"If you don't mind my sucky handwriting."

"I don't care. Those words on paper are like a piece of your personality. I can look at them and see you."

"Can't I just text you with a bunch of happy faces?"

"No way! I hate those little emoticons. It reminds me of the girls in junior high who would sprinkle them everywhere, like after every sentence. That and twenty-two exclamation points."

"I'd much rather call than write," he said.

"We can do that too," I said. "But while we're both staying with our parents, we won't always have privacy. I know my dad's going to be scrutinizing everything I do."

Conversation dwindled again as we closed in on the Utah Valley and turned onto Interstate 15 at Spanish Fork. I looked over at Chris, who seemed to be sleeping. But then I noticed a telltale reflection on his cheek.

"Chris?"

He didn't respond.

"Chris. You okay?"

He turned to me, dragging a sleeve across his moist eyes.

"It's okay, Chris. We're going to be okay." I reached for his left hand and kissed it.

He smiled. A sad smile.

"Whatever happens, I'll be here for you," I assured him. "I'll write you every week, and as soon as you get a phone, we'll be texting and talking as often as you need."

He nodded and wiped his eyes again. "I know."

"Six weeks will be gone before you know it, and we'll have a cute little apartment in Boise." I kissed Chris's hand again. "C'mon. Cheer up."

Chris smiled.

A short time later, we were passing the freeway exit signs for Provo and BYU.

"You know, out of thirty thousand students," he said, staring out the window toward Provo and Mount Timpanogos, which dominated the Wasatch backdrop, "most of them returned missionaries, there's got to be a lot of others like us, don't you think? I mean, what are the odds?"

"I'm sure there are," I said. "But most of them have probably kept it hidden. I mean, I haven't heard of any others who actually hooked up in the mission field. That's gotta be pretty rare."

"Yeah, but I bet there are a lot who wanted to."

I laughed. "Oh yeah, you'd better believe it."

Provo, Orem, and American Fork sped past, and we were finally crossing Point of the Mountain. The Salt Lake Valley spread out before us northward as far as the eye could see. To the east, the Wasatch Range grew ever more imposing, climaxing at Mount Olympus, which was already capped with snow.

"Mordor!" I announced in the voice of Strider.

But Chris didn't laugh. He only sighed.

"C'mon," I encouraged, "you can do this. Just keep looking ahead. Think of Boise."

"I know," Chris said. "I just dread facing my father. I'd rather face a church court than see the disappointment in his face."

"It was hard to see my dad deal with it too."

"You know, I'd be happier if he yelled at me, used a few swearwords, even. I could handle that. But no, he'll stare at me, shake his head, and wonder aloud how I could let him down, how I could disgrace the family and all that."

"It sucks, I know," I empathized. "Sometimes I think Mormons shouldn't be so passive. It's not natural. You know? People need to blow off steam to stay sane. We should get angry more often. It'd be healthier."

"Maybe that's why there are so many Mormons on Prozac," he said.

"Really. Did you ever read *Angels in America*?"

He turned to me. "Yes!" he said with sudden excitement. "I thought I was the only Mormon who did!"

"Nope. I did too," I said. "And I knew a girl in my home ward who did too. We'd sometimes talk about it after Sunday school."

"I didn't have anybody to discuss it with," Chris said. "It was confusing because, for one, I was only fifteen. And it kept jumping all over from the Jewish woman, to the creepy old lawyer with AIDS, then to the gay guy and the angel."

"Yeah, it was hard to follow. But my favorite was the housewife on Prozac who would go into the refrigerator and hallucinate, talking to the angel."

"Oh yeah, she was pretty funny," he said.

"But I think sometimes, even though they made her out to be crazy, she often made the most sense."

I was happy to keep Chris distracted with conversation, but eventually neither of us could escape the weight of the burden we felt as we approached the heart of Salt Lake City. We were both silent as I took the freeway exit at Sixth South. One block before State Street, where we would be turning north, I saw what I'd been looking for and turned south on Main.

"Hey, wrong way," Chris said.

I made an immediate left into a parking lot and pulled up in front of the AT&T store. I shut off the engine and turned to him. "We're getting you a cell phone before I let you go."

"I…. You don't have to do that," he protested. "My dad will get me set up in the next couple of days. Really."

"You think I'm going to wait a couple of days to call or text you?"

"It's not that long," he countered.

"Look," I said, taking his hand in my own and stroking his wrist, "I've been blessed to have had your company every single day for the last four months. Three days would be an eternity without talking to you. I'd be going through withdrawal."

Chris smiled and gave me a peck on the cheek. "You're sweet."

After purchasing Chris a pay-as-you-go phone, we headed north on State Street when I made another turn Chris wasn't expecting, this time onto Fourth South. "Another errand?" he asked.

"Kind of," I said. "I just remembered something we forgot to do."

"What?"

I just smiled.

"Are you gonna tell me?"

"You'll see."

A minute later I spotted it and pulled into a driveway. I headed straight for the drive-through window.

Chris let out a laugh.

"Eat Taco Bell!" we shouted in unison.

Chris rolled his eyes upward. "Rodney, this is for you."

We sat in the parking lot eating our meal. We reminisced about Rodney for a while, then fell into silence.

When we pulled back onto State Street fifteen minutes later, approaching Temple Square, I said, "Okay, so I know it's somewhere up near the Capitol, right?"

"Yeah," Chris said. "Ensign Peak, actually. Just stay on State until you run into the Capitol, then turn right and keep going up."

As we passed the temple, I made a show of looking up toward the twenty-eight-story Church Office Building opposite. "You know, I think I see the Eye of Sauron up there."

Chris gave a bitter laugh. "You're not far off, you know. There are no secrets in this town. Everybody is watching everybody else. It's a den of snitches and gossips. I hate it. Everybody always knows everybody else's business."

"I don't think that's just Salt Lake. The church is like that everywhere."

"Yeah, well, when they get an earful of what I've been up to lately, they're gonna wet their panties."

I laughed and looked at Chris lovingly. "I'm really gonna miss you, you know that, right?"

"Yeah. Me too. I mean…."

"Yeah, I know what you mean."

"Okay, turn left here, and then left again. You can just let me out at the end of the street."

"What? I don't get to see where the esteemed Elder Noah G. Merrill lives?"

Chris rolled his eyes. "It's a gated community. I've got to call and have somebody come get me."

I whistled. We had just reached the gates at the end of the cul-de-sac. The sign read "Dorchester Pointe." Beyond us the entire Salt Lake Valley, from the south end of the lake down to the Point of the Mountain, and the entire Wasatch Front lay spread out before us. "Wow! This is amazing! I can't believe you live here."

"Believe me, I'd give my right arm to live a little less conspicuously," Chris said as I pulled the Blazer to a stop.

Chris hopped out and went around back to start gathering his things. I followed and helped. When his belongings were all in a pile at the curb beside the gate, he and I turned to each other. As if on cue, tears sprang from both of us.

"Oh my God," I said, my voice breaking. "This is gonna be a lot harder than I thought."

"I know," Chris said in a wavering voice.

I wanted to throw my arms around him and not let go, but I was conscious of where we were standing, and I knew better than to try. Like it or not, Chris had to live here for the time being, and it would be selfish of me to set tongues to wagging for a moment of gratification.

And so we stood, about two feet apart, staring into each other's eyes, crying. I didn't know how long it was, only that it wasn't long enough.

Chris slowly pulled out his new phone, turned it on, and then paused. "Well," he said, looking at me one more time, "this is it." And then he dialed.

Seconds elapsed. "Hello, Mom?" Chris said into the phone. "Yeah, it's me. I'm here at the gate. Can you come get me?"

EPILOGUE

FOUR MONTHS, two weeks, three days. And now the road trip was over.

My reunion with my family was anticlimactic, really. My father never mentioned the road trip, and he asked no questions on the few occasions someone else brought it up. In private, I told my mother about the best moments of the trip, but even she got uncomfortable when I spoke of Chris in a loving tone. I didn't do it to make a scene, but I couldn't hide how I felt; it was a part of who I was now.

I wrote Chris a long letter the very night I returned home. I was tempted to call him but decided to give him some space to deal with his own family drama. Chris had my number and could call if he needed someone to talk to. I was able to cry on Mary Anne's shoulder when I needed to, and she didn't judge me over my love for Chris. But since she was attending BYU-Idaho, I knew there was a limit to what she could be seen to tolerate in that environment.

As the days grew into weeks, and there was still no word from Chris, I began to get fidgety. I began calling him several times a week but always got voice mail. When the weeks became months, I became despondent, fearing the worst. Either he had changed his mind—which I refused to believe was possible—or someone had changed it for him. How could we have been blind to that risk? Noah Merrill was a General Authority; of course he'd try to put Chris into reparative therapy! That was the church's modus operandi.

I continued to send letters, pouring out my soul to Chris, even though I had no way of knowing if they were reaching him. In a way, I hoped if someone else was reading them, they would understand the depth of my love for Chris. At times, I would insert passages into the letter that were meant primarily for some unseen snoop; I imagined it to be Noah Merrill himself. I would recount at length the beauty and spiritual nature of the love we shared on the road, just to drive the point home. It was also a plea to Chris, if he should actually be reading the letters, to remember what we had. I always ended my letters with, *I love you so much, Chris. Call me.*

By the time I left for school in Boise, Chris's cell number was no longer in service. By the time my first term ended, I stopped sending the weekly letters as well. My grieving had finally come to an end. It was time to move on.

I continued to carry Chris in my heart, though. It was impossible to extract him completely; he'd become a part of me. In my journal, I would reflect on the happy times we had shared and try not to focus on the loss. Eventually I learned to find happiness without Chris. I only hoped wherever Chris was now, he had found happiness too.

JON GARCIA is an accomplished musician and filmmaker. He is a graduate of Portland State University in Portland, Oregon with a BA in Film Studies and minor in Women Studies. In his music career, he has recorded two studio albums, a self-titled debut album in 2009 that circulated through BBC radio and acquired a following here in the states and overseas, and *The Lake*, which did very well in the UK and received rave reviews in the US and abroad. In 2009, Garcia released his first film, Tandem Hearts, about Portland, Oregon, transplants and the music scene at that time. In 2010 his film *The Falls* was released and acquired international distribution and was in film festivals all over the world. A year later, a sequel was released and once again received international attention. Currently Garcia is working on the paranormal thriller, *The Hours Till Daylight*, and a novel series to follow up *The Falls*.

MARTY BEAUDET has worked in communications for three decades as a novelist, screenwriter, editor, journalist, and actor. In addition to coauthoring *The Falls*, he has three published works: *By a Thread*, *Losing Addison*, and *Senseless Confidential*.

More from DSP Publications

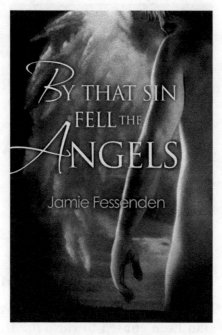

It begins with a 3:00 a.m. telephone call. On one end is Terry Bachelder, a closeted teacher. On the other, the suicidal teenage son of the local preacher. When Terry fails to prevent disaster, grief rips the small town of Crystal Falls apart.

At the epicenter of the tragedy, seventeen-year-old Jonah Riverside tries to make sense of it all. Finding Daniel's body leaves him struggling to balance his sexual identity with his faith, while his church, led by the Reverend Isaac Thompson, mounts a crusade to destroy Terry, whom Isaac believes corrupted his son and caused the boy to take his own life.

Having quietly crushed on his teacher for years, Jonah is determined to clear Terry's name. That quest leads him to Eric Jacobs, Daniel's true secret lover, and to get involved in Eric's plan to shake up their small-minded town. Meanwhile, Rev. Thompson struggles to make peace between his religious convictions and the revelation of his son's homosexuality. If he can't, he leaves the door open to eternal damnation—and for a second tragedy to follow.

www.dsppublications.com

More from DSP Publications

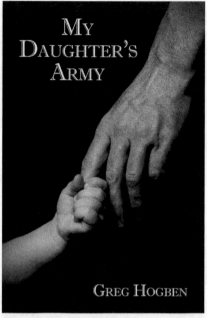

Has a gay man been chosen to raise the Daughter of God? Or is Adam Goodwin's adopted daughter plagued by a benevolent delusion that threatens to undermine her global campaign for women's rights?

From the moment Adam Goodwin discovered baby Sera abandoned in Grand Central Station, they shared an unexplainable bond. Sera grows into a compassionate and charismatic young woman, despite Adam's worries that she may have difficulty distinguishing fantasy from reality. Does her hypersensitivity to the suffering of others show compassion—or troubling obsession?

Adam channels Sera's growing fixation on gender inequality into uniting her army of social media followers to battle the worldwide oppression of women. But the encouragement he hoped would alleviate the symptoms of a possible mental illness only appear to make matters worse. The stress and success of her crusade seem to have brought on a mental break when she confides that she believes she is the female Messiah, sent to redress the injustices women face.

With enemies of her cause multiplying, Adam must protect Sera from the threats they pose—and from the threat she may pose to herself.

More from DSP Publications

Since the loss of his lively, charming wife to cancer six years ago, minister Paul Tobit has been operating on autopilot, performing his religious duties by rote. Everything changes the day he enters the church lobby and encounters a radiant, luminous being lit from behind, breathtakingly beautiful and glowing with life. An angel. For a moment Paul is so moved by his vision that he is tempted to fall on his knees and pray.

Even after he regains his focus and realizes he simply met a flesh-and-blood young man, Paul cannot shake his sense of awe and wonder. He feels an instant and overwhelming attraction for the young man, which puzzles him even as it fills his thoughts and fires his feelings. Paul has no doubt that God has spoken to him through this vision, and Paul must determine what God is calling him to do.

Thus begins a journey that will inspire Paul's ministry but put him at odds with his church as he is forced to examine his deeply held beliefs and assumptions about himself, his community, and the nature of love.

www.dsppublications.com

More from DSP Publications

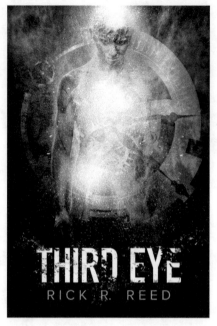

Who knew that a summer thunderstorm and his lost little boy would conspire to change single dad Cayce D'Amico's life in an instant? With Luke missing, Cayce ventures into the woods near their house to find his son, only to have lightning strike a tree near him, sending a branch down on his head. When he awakens the next day in the hospital, he discovers he has been blessed or cursed—he isn't sure which—with psychic ability. Along with unfathomable glimpses into the lives of those around him, he's getting visions of a missing teenage girl.

When a second girl disappears soon after the first, Cayce realizes his visions are leading him to their grisly fates. Cayce wants to help, but no one believes him. The police are suspicious. The press wants to exploit him. And the girls' parents have mixed feelings about the young man with the "third eye."

Cayce turns to local reporter Dave Newton and, while searching for clues to the string of disappearances and possible murders, a spark ignites between the two. Little do they know that nearby, another couple—dark and murderous—are plotting more crimes and wondering how to silence the man who knows too much about them.

www.dsppublications.com

More from DSP Publications

GNOMON

LUCHIA DERTIEN

Emile Delaurier is a beautiful militant revolutionary, a living beacon of righteous justice for the world. For Renaire, an artist in a constant battle against the demons in the bottle, it was obsession at first sight. His devotion led to two years of homicidal partnership as Renaire followed Delaurier in his ruthless quest for equality through the death of the corrupt, like a murderous Robin Hood.

Then Delaurier breaks his pattern, leading Renaire into Russia to kill a reporter with no immoral background, and gives no explanation for his actions.

When Interpol contacts Renaire, he already has enough problems—keeping Delaurier alive, dealing with the shift in their relationship, and surviving the broken past that still haunts him. But when he learns what Interpol wants from him, Renaire must face the truth about Delaurier: that a noble man isn't always a good one. He's left with a choice no man should ever have to make—to follow his heart or his morals.

www.dsppublications.com

More from DSP Publications

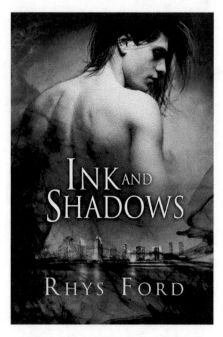

Kismet Andreas lives in fear of the shadows.

For the young tattoo artist, the shadows hold more than darkness. He is certain of his insanity because the dark holds creatures and crawling things only he can see—monsters who hunt out the weak to eat their minds and souls, leaving behind only empty husks and despair.

And if there's one thing Kismet fears more than being hunted—it's the madness left in its wake.

The shadowy Veil is Mal's home. As Pestilence, he is the youngest—and most inexperienced—of the Four Horsemen of the Apocalypse, immortal manifestations resurrected to serve—and cull—mankind. Invisible to all but the dead and insane, the Four exist between the Veil and the mortal world, bound to their nearly eternal fate. Feared by other immortals, the Horsemen live in near solitude but Mal longs to know more than Death, War and Famine.

Mal longs to be… more human. To interact with someone other than lunatics or the deceased.

When Kismet rescues Mal from a shadowy attack, Pestilence is suddenly thrust into a vicious war—where mankind is the prize, and the only one who has faith in Mal is the human the other Horsemen believe is destined to die.

www.dsppublications.com

More from DSP Publications

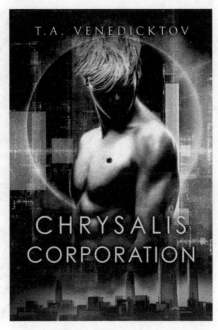

Together, they can change the rules of the galaxy and the definition of humanity.

When Damion Hawk is offered an opportunity to escape the destitute life of a miner on Mars and become an elite Alpha Fighter pilot, he jumps at the chance. Within the Chrysalis Corporation, Damion must learn to work with his Core—a man with computerized implants, no human emotions—and no rights. But unlike other Fighters, Damion can't treat Core 47 as a tool. He sees 47 as more than a machine, and he'll take deadly risks to help 47 find the humanity inside him.

Fighters and Cores are designed to work together and enhance each other's strengths in defense of their employer. Damion and 47 will need each other's support as suspicions about the all-powerful Chrysalis Corporation arise. Someone wants Damion and 47 gone, and they need to find out who and why while hiding 47's growing emotions and the love forming between them. If they can succeed, they might save not only themselves, but all Cores enslaved by the Corporation.

www.dsppublications.com

More from DSP Publications

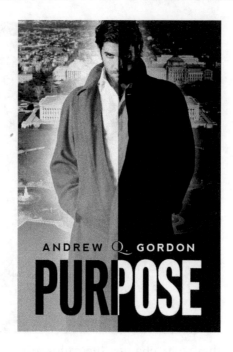

Forty years ago the Spirit of Vengeance—a Purpose—took William Morgan as its host, demanding he avenge the innocent by killing the guilty. Since then Will has retreated behind Gar, a façade he uses to avoid dealing with what he's become. Cold, impassive, and devoid of emotion, Gar goes about his life alone—until his tidy, orderly world is upended when he meets Ryan, a broken young man cast out by his family. Spurred to action for reasons he can't understand, Gar saves Ryan from death and finds himself confronted by his humanity.

Spending time with Ryan helps Will claw out from under Gar's shadow. He recognizes Ryan is the key to his reclaiming his humanity and facing his past. As Will struggles to control the Purpose, Ryan challenges him to rethink everything he knew about himself and the spirit that possesses him. In the process, he pushes Will to do something he hasn't done in decades: care.

www.dsppublications.com

More from DSP Publications

All sixteen-year-old Alex Nevus wants is to be two years older and become his sister Alice's legal guardian. That, and he'd like his first kiss, preferably with Jerod Haynes, the straight boy with the beautiful girlfriend and the perfect life. Sadly, wanting something and getting it are very different. Strapped with a mentally ill mother, Alex fears for his own sanity. Having a fairy on his shoulder only he can see doesn't help, and his mom's schizophrenia places him and Alice in constant jeopardy of being carted back into foster care.

When Alex's mother goes missing, everything falls apart. Frantic, he tracks her to a remote corner of Manhattan and is transported to another dimension—the land of the Unsee, the realm of the Fey. There he finds his mother held captive by the power-mad Queen May and learns he is half-human and half-fey—a Haffling.

As Alex's human world is being destroyed, the Unsee is being devoured by a ravenous mist. Fey are vanishing, and May needs to cross into the human world. She needs something only Alex can provide, and she will stop at nothing to possess it… to possess him.

www.dsppublications.com

For more
great fiction
from

DSP PUBLICATIONS

visit us online.

WWW.DSPPUBLICATIONS.COM